"Why so anxious to leave?"

Allan questioned her softly, his hands on her shoulders. "Here we are, after all this time, having a friendly, civilized chat, and you want to run away again."

"Don't, Allan, please." Beth's skin prickled, and she began to shiver. He drew her inexorably toward him. "Remember, Beth?" he whispered, lowering his head. Unable to help herself, she closed her eyes. His lips were warm and infinitely gentle.

"Remember," he repeated hoarsely, a command, not a question. His arm tightened, crushing the breath out of her. Then, with paralyzing suddenness, he thrust her away. Still caught up in the emotional turmoil he had unleashed, Beth swayed toward him.

Slowly, deliberately, Allan wiped his mouth with the back of his hand. It was like a slap across the face. "Damn you," he whispered, and strode away.

Dana James lives with her husband and three children in a converted barn on the edge of a Cornish village. She has written thrillers, historical romances and doctor-nurse romances but is now concentrating her efforts on writing contemporary romance fiction. In addition to extensive researching, which she adores, the author tries to write for a least four hours every day.

Books by Dana James

Don't miss any of our special offers. Write to us at the following address for information on our newest releases.

Harlequin Reader Service
901 Fuhrmann Blvd., P.O. Box 1397, Buffalo, NY 14240
Canadian address: P.O. Box 603,
Fort Erie, Ont. L2A 5X3

Snowfire
Dana James

Harlequin Books

TORONTO • NEW YORK • LONDON
AMSTERDAM • PARIS • SYDNEY • HAMBURG
STOCKHOLM • ATHENS • TOKYO • MILAN

Original hardcover edition published in 1988
by Mills & Boon Limited

ISBN 0-373-02973-X

Harlequin Romance first edition April 1989

CHAPTER ONE

BETH grasped the aluminium case containing her precious cameras in one hand and picked up her suitcase in the other.

Pausing a moment as the Icelandair shuttle took off again from Akureyri for Reykjavik, she looked up at the western slopes of the snow-capped mountain ridge rising majestically behind the town which jutted like a stubby finger into the fjord.

The snow, like sugar frosting on an enormous cake, glittered pale gold in the evening sun. It would still be shining at midnight. Should she take just one more shot?

Resisting the impulse, Beth curbed a smile. Apart from being perilously low on film, she could already hear Oliver's weary complaint. 'Not *another* sunset, Beth.'

Oliver was a marvellous agent who had obtained some terrific assignments for her. But they had frequent clashes over the kinds of pictures clients wanted for their travel brochures, press releases, guide books and nature calendars.

Oliver favoured what he called *practical* pictures of familiar subjects. Play it safe was his motto, using close-ups of flowers and animals, scenes of fishing boats in harbours, and modern hotels making sure to show the swimming-pool.

But Beth preferred trying to capture the mood of a place: morning mist over a mirror-smooth lake, the curve of a wave crashing on to shingle, cloud effects, sand shapes at ebb tide, the texture of rock, sun and shadows.

Discussions were often heated, but both recognised the need for compromise, so Oliver was able to keep Beth supplied with work, while she restricted her atmospheric shots to her private portfolio. She never travelled anywhere without the

battered brown zip-up case containing what she considered her
best work, photographs she had taken in her own time and at
her own expense. For some she had waited many hours to get
exactly the right light. Others had necessitated lying or
crouching, stiff and cramped, until a particular bird or animal
had lost its shyness and ignored her.

These shots, she knew, revealed far more artistry and talent
than anything she had ever done for Oliver and his clients.
One day she would prove her true worth as a photographer.
She was young yet, only twenty-five. In the meantime she
would do her best within the limits she had been set.

No one had it all. She thought of Hofi and Gunnar, the
friends she was going to stay with. Their marriage was rock-
solid. Gunnar's knowledge of this forty-thousand-square-mile
island and his ability as a mechanic had made him much
sought after by specialist tour operators and expedition
planners. With Hofi's organisational skills and gift of being
able to conjure up a hot, nourishing meal within minutes at
any time of day or night, they made a formidable team. Their
business was thriving. Yet what they longed for most, a child,
had so far eluded them.

As for herself, she had an absorbing and satisfying career,
and a growing reputation. She ate, drank and slept work.
There wasn't a moment to spare. No time even to contemplate
marriage or children. She made quite sure of that.

Beth squared her shoulders and took a firmer grip on her
case. Deliberately turning her thoughts outward, she
marvelled at the sharp clarity of the air. Almost all the heat for
industry and domestic use was obtained from hot springs and
superheated steam venting from the volcanoes that dotted the
country. So there was no smoke from coal or peat fires to
pollute the pristine atmosphere.

However, though it was the beginning of July, this northern
capital of Iceland lay just below the arctic circle, and the rising
wind had a keen edge to it. Beth was glad of her peach-

coloured padded jacket.

She had just spent a week in the south and each day this strange land of contrasts and surprises had offered something new and unexpected for her to capture on film. So much so that, despite bringing twice as much as she had intended to use, it had nearly all gone.

She walked briskly out of the little airport and looked round for a taxi. A noisy little Fiat squealed to a halt a few yards away. The door flew open and statuesque woman wearing a thick woollen sweater with the traditional design of grey, black and cream, unfolded long, red-trousered legs and hurried towards Beth, arms outstretched as she beamed a welcome. Her yellow-gold hair swung in a heavy braid over one shoulder.

'Hofi!' Beth exclaimed in surprise and delight. 'I didn't expect you to come and pick me up. I told you on the phone I'd get a taxi.'

'Now there is no need,' Hofi replied in her gentle sing-song voice. Taking Beth's suitcase, she heaved it into the back of the car. 'Did you use up all your film?'

Beth didn't reply, pulling a wry face.

'I knew it,' Hofi chuckled. 'Did I not warn you? We will stop and get more.'

Beth climbed in beside her. 'There can't be anything I haven't photographed,' she protested. 'Anyway, it's hideously expensive here, and besides, as from now I'm supposed to be on holiday. I really don't think——'

'Believe me,' Hofi promised as she started the car, 'you will need it.'

The noisy engine made conversation almost impossible, so after ascertaining that Gunnar was well and business was fine, Beth was content to look out of the window at the flat pasture land, the outer fields dotted with cattle, sheep and hardy little Icelandic horses, a vivid contrast to the bare brown rock of the scree-sloped mountains behind.

After making a detour to pick up more film, the cost of which had her doing frantic mental calculations as she handed over what seemed to be an awful lot of krona while Hofi added yet more boxes to the pile, they eventually arrived at the cream-painted house with its bright red roof.

Alongside, a Land Rover was parked outside a building that doubled as workshop, garage and store. Hofi switched off the engine but, as Beth started to get out, placed a restraining hand on her arm.

'When must you return to London?'

Beth shrugged. 'I was going at the end of the week. Three days with you will give me a chance to unwind and catch up on all your news. I know this is your busy season and I don't want to be in the way or outstay my welcome.'

'That is not possible,' Hofi smiled at her. 'You were with us only a few days last time, and this trip you have already been in Iceland a week before you come up to see us. I know,' Hofi cut her off, pressing her arm as Beth started to explain. 'But we love to have you with us. I do not ask because I want you to *go*. If there is no work waiting for you, I think you will wish to stay. But, if you *do* stay, there will be no time for relaxing or a holiday.'

Beth stared at her friend, noting the gleam of excitement in her eyes. 'Hofi, what *are* you talking about?'

'An expedition.' Hofi's attempt to be casual didn't quite come off. 'Across the lava fields and desert of the interior.' She paused, knowing she had Beth's complete attention. 'To the hot springs and ice caves beneath the Vatnajökull glacier,' she finished in quiet triumph.

'*What?*' Beth gasped. 'But I didn't think tourists were allowed——'

'This is not a trip for tourists,' Hofi explained. 'It is a scientific expedition. All the permits are arranged. We are taking geologists out to join the main party already on Vatnajökull.'

'What is happening on the glacier?' Beth could hardly contain all the questions clamouring to be asked. 'What are they doing up there?'

'They are waiting for a glacier burst. It is five years since the last bad one, and it seems they have much equipment on the ice-cap which tells them that the pressure of water melted by the Grímsvöten volcano is now so high that a burst could occur very soon.'

Beth stared blindly ahead.

'There will be seven in the party,' Hofi went on. 'Eight if you will join us. I have suggested to Mr Brennan, who is funding this part of the expedition, that you could be the party's official photographer. He said he would think it over. But in any case I told him I would need some help with the cooking. Beth, you must come.'

Beth flinched, quickly turning her head away. *Assistant cook and photographer.* The pain was still as raw and fierce as it had been almost two years ago.

Working in Switzerland on a fashion shoot for ski wear, she had desperately wanted some shots of the Rhône glacier, but had been unable to persuade anyone to take her.

Thanks to an untimely tumble on the nursery slopes resulting in a broken ankle for the assistant cook from a geological survey team, she had managed to get herself accepted in his place. She had got her pictures. And she had met Allan.

Allan Bryce, the first, the only man she had ever loved. The man she had married, except it had not been a marriage at all. The man who had broken her heart and destroyed her trust. Had it not been for her work——

'Beth?' Hofi sounded puzzled and concerned.

Shaking off the unexpected and pain-filled recollection, Beth stretched her mouth into a smile. 'Just try and keep me away.'

Deeply immersed in keeping a flood of other memories at bay, it did not occur to Beth to wonder why Hofi, who had cooked single-handed for parties of ten or more, should need an assistant for an expedition of eight.

Gradually her smile became less strained, more genuine, as reality sank in. 'Hofi, this is fantastic. It's the chance of a lifetime.'

'Yes,' Hofi said with sudden seriousness, 'and you must not waste it, Beth.'

Beth dived out of the car and reached into the back for her cases and leather shoulder-bag. 'No chance of that.' She grinned over her shoulder. 'I'll convince this Mr Brennan he can't possibly manage without me. You're a wonderful friend, Hofi.'

'I hope so,' Hofi murmured as she led the way into the house.

The smell of fresh coffee made Beth's mouth water, reminding her she had not eaten for almost six hours.

Hofi dropped Beth's suitcase at the bottom of the wide, open-plan staircase. 'Come and meet the others before I show you to your room.'

Beth's eyes widened. 'They're *all* staying here?'

Hofi grinned. 'Four weeks ago we took a party of bird-watchers to Myvatn. There were ten of them and I had to give them supper and put them all up the night before we left. In a way it's easier. At least we know everyone has arrived and we can get them moving early. They don't realise how important it is in Iceland to start any journey, even short ones, in the morning, to allow for sudden changes in river conditions or the weather. At least this time we did not have to give up our room. But,' she looked apologetic, 'I'm afraid you'll have to share. Do you mind?'

Beth smothered her dismay. 'Of course not. That's all part of an expedition.' Yet she could not help wishing she had had just one night of complete relaxation. The past week had been hectic, involving a lot of travel and very long hours. And the sudden memories of Allan had been deeply unsettling. At least there was no chance of their paths crossing here. According to the *Natural World* magazine, Dr Allan Bryce was on the Hubbard glacier in Alaska. She had bought the magazine because it contained several of her own shots of alpine flowers growing through snow. Seeing his name had caused a peculiar wrenching sensation in her stomach. She would learn to overcome it, and control her reactions. She *had* to. Still, she comforted herself, this *was* the chance of a lifetime. Sharing a room was a small price to pay.

'I expect we'll be two to a tent as well.'

Hofi nodded, her relief obvious. 'I knew you would understand. I has some difficulty explaining it to Miss Brennan. She did not seem to understand that there is no room in the Land Rover for anything but essentials, and that to have a tent each was just not possible.

Beth shook her head. 'I don't know how you hang on to your patience.'

Hofi shrugged. 'People are very understanding . . . usually. But sometimes it takes a while.' They exchanged a knowing grin. Then she opened the door.

After the crushing anonymity of hotel rooms the welcoming warmth and familiarity were like a homecoming for Beth. One brief glance told her that the mellow wood, comfortable armchairs and sofas, glowing wall-lights and heavy-weave curtains were all just as she remembered.

The two men and a woman sitting in one corner of the large low-beamed room had stopped their conversation and were viewing Beth with a mixture of interest and curiosity.

Hofi began, 'This is Beth——'

'Farrell,' Beth put in quickly. She had told Hofi about reverting to her maiden name when she was here last time and she didn't want any mistakes or slip-ups. Ridiculous it might be, but even hearing Allan's name hurt.

A short, stocky man of about sixty with grizzled hair and shaggy eyebrows hauled himself out of the depths of a leather armchair and swept Beth with an appraising stare. 'I guess you must be this here photographer Mizz Petursson told us about.'

Beth glanced uncertainly at Hofi. 'Miss Petursson?'

Hofi bit her lip, masking a smile. 'He means me,' she whispered. She turned to the man. 'I am Hofi, Mr Brennan. In Iceland women do not take their husband's name when they marry.'

A frown deepened the furrows on his lined forehead. 'God-damm it, more of that Women's Liberation bull——'

'Eugene!' From the corner of the brightly cushioned sofa, a plump woman somewhere in her fifties, with strawberry-rinsed hair lacquered into a fluffy meringue, rolled her eyes at Beth and Hofi. 'My husband has a short fuse concerning certain matters.' She added in a whisper, 'He blames our daughter's second divorce on the Women's Movement.'

'Damn right I do,' Eugene Brennan grunted.

'He also tends to forget that other people are not always quite as,' she paused delicately, '*blunt* as he is. Now, Eugene,' she scolded, though her soft drawl was patient and good-humoured, 'you just mind your language.' She smiled up at Beth, 'I'm Lucille Brennan,' then switched her gaze to Hofi. 'Tell me, dear, why don't you use your husband's name? I mean, it's not rude, or funny, or unpronounceable. You should hear some of the ones we have back home. I think Petursson is a real nice name.'

'Thank you.' Hofi was clearly touched by the woman's transparent niceness. 'I like it too. But here we do not have the family names. Petursson means simply son of Petur. A man's surname comes from his father's first name. My husband's father is called Arni Jonsson.'

'So he's the son of Jon?' Lucille ventured. 'Is it the same for women?'

Hofi nodded. 'I am Hofi Karlsdottir, the daughter of Karl. We address each other by our first names. That has been our custom since ancient times. It is not something new.'

'OK.' Eugene threw up his hands in surrender. 'If that's the way you do things here . . . ' He shook his head, but it was obvious to Beth, as she caught Hofi's eye, that he didn't really approve.

'Mr Brennan is from Texas,' Hofi said to Beth.

'Guess you didn't need tellin', did you, girl.'

Beth met the gimlet eyes almost hidden beneath untidy brows and realised at once that there was far more to Eugene Brennan than his brash outspokenness and colourful outfit of red plaid shirt, blue and yellow golf sweater and navy tartan trousers suggested. 'What else do you do?' he demanded.

Beth wasn't sure what he meant. 'Besides what?'

'Besides takin' snapshots.'

'Nothing, Mr Brennan,' Beth replied, coolly polite. 'Photography is my . . . profession.' She had nearly said *my life*.

'Do you make a lot of money?'

She managed to hide her shock. He certainly did go straight to the point. Beth met his gaze levelly. 'I get by, Mr Brennan.'

'And are you good at it?'

'I'm better,' she replied quietly.

Eugene Brennan's eyes sharpened. There was a moment's silence. 'Just need the chance to prove it, eh?' She nodded and he stuck out his hand. 'Welcome aboard, girl.' His handshake was dry and firm. 'I started off in cattle, played the market and made a few bucks, now I can do what I *really* enjoy.'

Beth placed her camera case and bag on one of the chairs. 'What's that, Mr Brennan?'

'I guess you'd better call me Eugene, in deference to our hostess here. I like to travel. This here earth of ours just fascinates me. The mountains and valleys, jungles and rivers, volcanoes and glaciers. They're livin' history. I want to see 'em for myself. Geology's a hobby of mine. Never had no formal training, but I take it real serious. I guess I'm a lucky man. I can afford to do what I want, and I got me a wife who indulges my passion for the past.' He turned and smiled at Lucille.

Dressed in similar fashion to her husband, but with ostrich feather mules over her woollen socks, Lucille grimaced. 'Guess I do look like an old relic at that.' But there was no mistaking the humour and love in the glance she threw at her husband. 'You finished giving Miss Farrell the third degree, Eugene?' she chided.

'Call me Beth, please,' Beth insisted as she shook the woman's small, heavily-ringed hand.

'Gee, and I always thought you English girls were so formal.'

Lucille's soft drawl robbed the words of any offence.

Beth grinned and shrugged lightly. 'It's very difficult to remain formal on an expedition.'

'I certainly hope you're right.'

Beth looked up quickly. There was open interest on the pleasant face of the young man who had just spoken. He had been sprawled in the corner chair, but now stood at her shoulder. A few inches taller than her, his eyes held a combination of admiration and challenge that startled Beth. He stood so close she had no choice but to take the hand he proffered.

'Rob Wilson, thirty-one, single and house-trained. Generally well behaved but responsive to challenge, and thoroughly enjoys expeditions. I'm a geologist, by the way.' He held on to her hand a fraction longer than necessary. Beth pulled it gently but firmly free, making no effort to suppress the laughter in her voice.

'Is that an introduction or a commercial?'

He spread his hands. 'Communication is what it's all about.' The dancing light in his eye told Beth he wasn't entirely serious and, as a means of making an impression and being remembered, his greeting was both novel and amusing.

'I see,' Beth said in mock seriousness. 'Well, at least no one will ever accuse you of reticence, Mr Wilson.'

He looked aghast. 'Rob, please. No one has called me Mr Wilson for years, except my mother, but we were never close.'

Beth stared at him wide-eyed, then realised he was deliberately teasing. She shot him a dry look. 'My heart bleeds for you. However, you'll have to excuse me, I'd like to go and freshen up.' She picked up her camera case and bag.

Rob assumed a mournful expression and placed both hands over his heart. 'I shall count the seconds until your return,' he vowed.

Beth compressed her lips to keep from smiling. It wouldn't do to be too impressed. Rob Wilson might lack other qualities but aside from his sense of humour, ego wasn't one of them.

'Don't hold your breath,' Beth said kindly, and followed Hofi out.

Once outside the door she raised her brows at Hofi, whistling soundlessly and they both had to smother a fit of giggles.

'This is going to be some expedition,' Beth murmured behind Hofi as they went upstairs. 'Did you say there was a Miss Brennan?'

Hofi nodded, unable to hide a slight grimace as she pointed to the bathroom door behind which Beth could hear the sound of the shower running. 'Her father says she's very fit, she plays much tennis and does aerobics.' Hofi sounded doubtful and lowered her voice to a whisper. 'She is very pretty, but not, I think, a happy person.' She opened the door to the room Beth had stayed in during her last visit.

They stood on the threshold, speechless. The room looked as though it had been hit by a tornado. Two suitcases lay open on one of the single beds. Dresses, shirts, trousers and lacy underwear were strewn over both the cases and the other bed. Two cashmere sweaters lay in a heap where they had fallen on the floor. Three pairs of high-heeled shoes and a pair of obviously new walking-boots were scattered across the carpet, and the dressing-table groaned under its burden of face-cream, hand-cream, tissues, talc, a large make-up bag spilling innumerable shades of eye-shadow, blusher and lipstick on to the glass top, brushes, combs, and a set of Carmen rollers.

'When did the Brennans arrive?' Beth murmured incredulously.

'This afternoon.' Hofi was equally stunned. 'They were the first to come. I gave them coffee, then Miss Brennan came up here. She has not been down since.'

'And I'm sharing a tent with . . . this?' Beth groaned. She heaved a sigh. 'She might be fit, but it doesn't look as though Miss Brennan has much experience of packing for an expedition.'

'Her mother said she was not very keen to come,' Hofi admitted. 'But they felt it was not wise to leave her at home alone.'

Neither had taken their eyes from the mess. They were both mesmerised by the scale of chaos reached in such a short time.

'How old is she?' Beth murmured.

'Your age,' Hofi replied, 'twenty-five.'

'What?' Beth's head flew round. 'I thought we were talking about a child, a spoiled teenager. An *untidy* spoiled teenager.' She picked her way through the litter to the further of the two beds and, scooping up two wispy bras and several triangular scraps of lace joined by ribbon-covered elastic, tossed them on to the tangle of clothing spilling out of the cases. She dropped her camera case and her bag on the coverlet, then, with a shrug, gathered up an armful of the girl's clothes, and after a moment's hesitation, dumped them in a heap on the open cases, then took her own suitcase from Hofi.

'With two ex-husbands?' Hofi reminded her.

Beth caught her lip between her teeth. 'I'd forgotten about that. Do you think this might have contributed to . . .?' She gestured towards the mess.

Hofi shrugged. 'Who can tell? Perhaps this is just reaction.' She shook her head. 'Gunnar would beat me, I think.'

'Where is Gunnar?' Beth asked quickly, sensing danger in the direction the conversation was taking. Hofi was her closest friend, the only person in whom she had been able to confide her grief and sense of utter betrayal. Even that had been almost a year after it had happened. After she had opened the door and come face to face with the beautiful, dusky-skinned Shalana. A year in which she had tried so desperately to forget Allan Bryce, to wipe from her memory those four incredible, ecstatic months. But she had succeeded only in papering over the wound. It no longer showed. But it had not healed and even now, another year later, a name, a picture in a magazine, a smell, would snag like a thorn at her memory, and the pain was almost unbearable. Surely it would end soon? Time was suppose to heal all wounds. Well, why wasn't it healing hers?

'He—er—he had to go out.' Hofi seemed momentarily at a loss. 'He had to pick up the other Land Rover, and extra fuel,' she finished quickly, and glanced at her watch. 'He should be back soon. I must go and prepare the meal. There is still some packing to do before we set off in the morning. Do you have everything you need? I left a clean towel——' She frowned, then with the air of a conjurer, pulled it out from beneath the armful of clothes Beth had removed from her bed. 'Here it is. Come down as soon as you are ready. I want to know all you have been doing since you were here last time.'

Beth took off her padded jacket and dropped it on top of her camera case. Pushing long, slim fingers through her cropped hair, she rubbed the tension from her neck.

Was it her imagination, or were there undercurrents? Invisible tensions in Hofi she had not sensed before?

Unzipping her case, Beth gave a little shrug. Faced with the preparations and planning to cater for the comfort and well-being of eight people during the next week or ten days, Hofi was entitled to look a little strained. The fact that she had been doing the job with great success for several years did not lessen the amount of hard work, especially as each trip and expedition was made up of individuals, each one of whom considered their own likes, dislikes and requirements to be of paramount importance.

As she lifted out her toilet bag and pyjamas, Beth's mouth twisted wryly. Compared with the drift of snowy lace and silk on Miss Brennan's pillow, her own night attire looked decidedly unfeminine. She sighed. At least she'd be warm in her sleeping-bag, and that was what counted in a country where eleven per cent of the land was covered by glaciers and ice-fields and where the three-hundred-year 'Little Ice Age' had only ended at the beginning of this century.

Staring at the pink brushed cotton, Beth sank down on the edge of her bed. The pyjamas were only a small part of it, a symptom of something that went far deeper. Her wardrobe contained more pairs of jeans and cords than it did dresses. Of course, to a certain extent her work dictated her choice of clothes. No one would take seriously a wild-life and landscape photographer who turned up for a shoot in pencil skirt and six-inch heels.

Her gaze slid over the cosmetic-laden dressing-table then rose to study her reflection in the mirror. The only make-up *she* had on was a peach lip-gloss.

Beth observed herself critically, something she had not done for a very long time. She had a good colour, probably because of all the fresh air she got. It was one of the perks and problems of her chosen career, for it meant she was out in all weathers and got through moisturiser by the bucketful.

Thick, dark lashes fringed eyes that varied with her mood between green and hazel. Her nose was—just a nose, neither large nor small; it fitted her face well enough. She had not noticed the shadows beneath her eyes before, nor the faint lines of strain about her mouth.

Her dark brown hair, ruffled by the wind, was a feathery cap revealing small ears.

She could justify every aspect of her appearance, from her

cropped head, bottle-green cords, fawn shirt and the apricot sweater that underplayed her slender figure, to the walking-boots and thick socks on her small feet.

But what it all came down to in the end was the desire to win recognition for herself as a photographer, *but not to be noticed as a woman.*

The realisation, prompted by the interest and speculation in Rob Wilson's eyes, plus the amazing variety and gossamer delicacy of Miss Brennan's lingerie, came as a shock.

The door opened and Beth jerked round. Pretty, Hofi had said. But the girl who entered was not merely pretty, she was *gorgeous.*

White-blonde hair tumbled over the shoulders of a négligé of sapphire satin and cream lace. Tanned glowing skin, china-blue eyes, a small, beautifully modelled nose and full soft lips completed the picture. The figure beneath the belted satin was voluptuous, with high, full breasts and rounded hips separated by a small, neat waist. Both hands and feet were well cared for, with oval nails immaculately painted with pearl-pink varnish.

As she caught sight of Beth, the girl hesitated and a frown marred the smooth perfection of her forehead.

Feeling positively plain, Beth stood up, clutching the pink cotton pyjamas to her midriff. When she had leapt at Hofi's offer to be part of the expedition, she hadn't realised just what she would be letting herself in for. Hofi might have warned her. Miss Brennan with her wealthy father, two ex-husbands and film-star looks, was probably a first-class bitch who would make life hell for whoever was forced to share with her. Individual tents had never seemed so appealing as they did at this moment.

Beth swallowed her nervousness, mentally raising her defences. But before she could say anything, the other girl spoke.

'Gee, I'm so sorry about the mess.' Her voice was soft and husky and to her own astonishment, Beth found herself wondering if the cause was too many cigarettes, or too many tears. 'I'm not always quite so . . . ' she made a vague gesture '. . . well, maybe I am. I don't mean to be, it's just that things sorta . . . spread.' She gave a small, helpless shrug. Then, juggling her towel, toilet bag, a jar and two small ornate bottles into one hand, she smiled, revealing white, even teeth, and extended the other towards Beth. 'I'm Gaynor.' Her smile faltered for an instant. 'Gaynor Brennan,' she said, hauling the smile back into place.

Beth introduced herself. 'I hope you don't mind, I moved some of your things.'

'I guess you had to.' Gaynor pushed her hair back and stared at the clothes scattered about the room. 'I don't know how I'm going to get this stuff back into my cases. There seems a lot more than I remember.'

Beth's relief was enormous. The mess, and her first glimpse of the beautiful blonde, had prepared her for the worst, but there was a vulnerability about Gaynor, an air of bewilderment, that Beth found oddly touching.

But though one potential problem had been removed, the other still remained and would require careful handling.

'It's never easy, packing for a holiday,' Beth agreed. 'I read somewhere that you should make a list of the least you could get by on, then halve it. It's good advice, even though I don't always manage to stick to it.'

Gaynor dropped her towel on to the floor and added the other things to the mound on the dressing-table. 'Say, do we dress for dinner tonight?'

Beth shook her head quickly. 'No, we usually wear what we intend to travel in the following day. I'll be staying as I am.'

Gaynor nodded and began rummaging through the pile of clothing. 'Do you travel a lot?'

Beth smiled. 'I'm very lucky. My job takes me all over the world. I'm a photographer,' she added as Gaynor looked up questioningly, a dress in each hand.

'Gee, that's real interesting. You do fashion? Stuff like that?'

Beth shook her head, itching to rescue the crumpled jade silk-jersey Gaynor had tossed towards the foot of the bed and missed, which now lay in a heap on the floor. 'Not often. I specialise in wild-life studies, our natural world, that kind of thing.'

Gaynor's eyes widened and Beth could see her admiration was genuine. 'You must have a real talent. I guess there's a lot of competition.'

Beth shrugged. 'It's the same in most professions. A woman has to be twice as good as a man to be considered equal. But I'm lucky, I've got a marvellous agent. He deals with the clients, I just take the pictures.'

'You mean he has to play down the fact that you're a woman,' Gaynor observed sympathetically, and Beth warmed to the other girl's shrewd understanding.

'But it won't be like that for ever,' she said with quiet determination. 'I don't intend to do travel brochures and publicity stills for the rest of my life. That's why I'm over the moon about this trip. It's a fantastic opportunity to get some really rare shots.'

'Attagirl.' Gaynor winked at her. 'Look,' she gestured at the clothes, 'what do you suggest for——?'

Before she could complete the sentence, Beth had picked out a lilac Viyella shirt, purple trousers in a fine woollen flannel and a cream cashmere sweater. Her mind boggled as she worked out the probable cost of those items alone, and everything in Gaynor's cases was of similar quality.

'Do you have a warm jacket?' Beth asked. 'And you really should have waterproofs, a top and leggings. Plus hat and mittens. In case of blizzards,' she explained, seeing the blank look on Gaynor's face.

'But it's *July*,' Gaynor protested, her beautiful features registering dismay.

'That doesn't stop the snow.'

'I guess Poppa must have taken care of all that.' Reaching into the wardrobe, Gaynor passed Beth a jacket. It was of finest leather, the colour of milky coffee, and as soft and supple as velvet. Beth ran her palm over the fur lining and her eyes widened. Surely it couldn't be? But it was. *Mink*.

There was genuine concern in Gaynor's voice as she asked, 'Will that be OK?'

Beth had to fight a sudden urge to laugh. Gaynor would not understand, and Beth had no wish to hurt her feelings. She sensed that had happened all too often. 'It'll be fine,' she assured her, handing the jacket back and resolutely stamping on the tiny pang of envy.

'Look,' Beth began.

'Could I . . .' Gaynor said at exactly the same instant. Both stopped, laughing, and Beth gestured for Gaynor to continue.

'Well, I guess I've got a nerve, on such short acquaintance and all, but . . . you're the expert. Will you help me pack?'

Beth grinned at her. 'I thought you'd never ask.'

CHAPTER TWO

AN HOUR later they went down to supper, the packing finally complete. It had not been easy. Almost every item discarded by Beth had been retrieved by Gaynor with a cry of 'but I must have that,' or 'I can't possibly manage . . .' and even 'I *have* to take . . .' Without exception Beth made sure they went into the case which was remaining behind.

The large bag of beauty aids had been whittled down to what Gaynor pleaded were bare essentials. Beth had then removed moisture cream and lipstick and, placing them in Gaynor's hand, had put the rest into the storage case.

The greatest bone of contention had been the Carmen rollers. Gaynor's horror at the thought of being separated from them had exasperated Beth.

'For goodness' sake, I'm not asking you to cut off an arm or a leg!'

'You might as well,' Gaynor wailed. 'My hair is baby-fine. I have to curl it every day. If I don't I just look a total mess.'

With some difficulty Beth had eventually persuaded her that putting her hair up would solve the problems, and be more comfortable under a hat.

At last Gaynor conceded that time, and the facilities she had always taken for granted, would be severely restricted. Then a gleam of determination brightened her eyes, worrying Beth.

But Gaynor wasn't going back on her request for Beth's help, she had merely decided that if from tomorrow she had to look a wreck, tonight she would, as she put it, *give it the works*.

When Beth returned from a swift, refreshing shower,

23

Gaynor's blonde head was covered in neat rows of rollers and she watched, fascinated, as Gaynor wielded brushes of varying shapes and sizes with a professionalism born of long practice, stroking, shading and blending the subtle colours she selected from the rainbow range in her case.

After a critical, almost clinical, appraisal of the result, she unrolled her hair, then brushed, teased and sprayed it into a frothy cascade of waves and curls. Pushing the last tendril into place she turned to Beth. 'Well? What do you think?'

Beth shook her head in admiration. 'It's amazing. You don't actually look as if you're wearing make-up, and yet——'

'I know,' Gaynor nodded. 'The eyes seem larger, the cheekbones higher, the mouth soft and full-lipped.'

Beth was struck by the way she referred to her features so objectively, as if they belonged to someone else.

'But that's the whole point, isn't it,' Gaynor said with brittle gaiety, 'illusion.' She turned and looked at herself in the mirror. 'I'm an illusion,' and Beth was startled by the desolation in her tone.

Rob Wilson's eyes nearly popped out of his head as they slid past Beth to Gaynor, who acknowledged him with a polite nod and the merest suggestion of a smile, before crossing the room to where her parents sat on one of the sofas with drinks on a small table in front of them.

Without taking his eyes off Gaynor, Rob surreptitiously grabbed Beth's arm. 'Who is that?' he whispered, barely moving his lips.

Beth realised he must have arrived after Gaynor had taken herself upstairs.

'She's the Brennans' daughter. Her name is Gaynor. And she's a very nice person,' Beth found herself adding. She wasn't sure why. Except that behind the sophisticated, glossy exterior Beth had glimpsed sadness and uncertainty and didn't want to see Gaynor hurt more.

'I bet she is,' Rob breathed, and Beth knew he hadn't really taken in what she had said.

She felt a small pang. No one had ever ogled her like that, The brief envy quickly evaporated and she gave a mental shrug. She had never looked like that.

Recalling Gaynor's haunting reference to illusion, Beth wondered if perhaps there wasn't a high price to pay for being beautiful.

'Shall I introduce you?' Beth offered. 'Not that you need my assistance.' She couldn't resist teasing him. 'You managed quite well on your own with me.'

'That was different,' he said absently. As Beth's brows climbed he realised what he had said and how it had sounded. 'Oh, God,' he looked at her in concern, 'I'm sorry, I didn't mean——'

'It's quite all right,' Beth smiled, sympathising with the rush of colour to his face.

'It isn't that you're not really very attractive,' he hurried on, 'you are. But she . . . ' He trailed off, words failing him.

'Is *stunning?*' Beth supplied in a whisper.

Rob gaped at her, then nodded, his expression suddenly serious. 'A girl like that . . . hell . . . ' he glanced at Beth and confessed, 'it saps a bloke's confidence.'

Incredulity widened Beth's eyes.

He shrugged, struggling to explain. 'I mean, just look at her.' He sounded awestruck. 'She'd probably chew me up and spit out the pieces.'

Beth felt a swift surge of anger. 'How can you say that? You don't even know her. That's a *person* you're talking about. Not some sort of monster or a wind-up doll. Yes, she's lovely. She's also a human being. With the same worries and feelings as the rest of us.' Beth quickly controlled herself, glimpsing the surprise on Rob's face, wondering herself at her protectiveness towards Gaynor, then realising its source.

Having known pain herself, she recognised it in the other girl.

Rob's eyes flicked towarsd the lovely blonde, then back at Beth. He looked dubious. 'She looks a picture of self-possession to me.'

'We all have a face we present to the world,' Beth replied, thinking of her facade. She was the busy career girl with no time or inclination for relationships which tried to progress beyond the casual. That was the proctective shell into which she had retreated, waiting for the wounds to heal, sometimes wondering in despair if they ever would.

For Allan had been the first, the yardstick by which she would, however unwittingly, measure every other man. And despite the way it had ended, despite hating him for the ruthless cynicism with which he had shattered her life, no one she had met since had even begun to compare. Or was it that she had not given them the chance? Keeping them at a distance, fighting shy of involvement, of any contact beyond the lightest kiss, she had earned herself the label of frigid, and worse.

But she wasn't. How many nights had she prayed for the oblivion of sleep to release her from the tormenting memories of his hard-muscled body covering hers, both of them dewed with sweat, his gentle, knowing hands, the kisses and caresses that touched the very core of her womanhood, drawing her to the summit of ecstasy? His strong arms enfolding her as the world silently exploded and, clinging to him with a wordless cry, she was falling . . . falling . . . drowning in pulsing waves of sensastion that carried them both to a far-off shore, where they lay entwined, safe in their own secret island of peace and contentment.

But even sleep denied her a refuge. For he was there, at the edge of her dreams, waiting. *Would she never be free of him?*

'You think I should?' Rob's tone was a mixture of doubt and hope.

Shamed by her thoughts, shaken by the vividness of her recollection, and vastly relieved that Rob was far too immersed in his own problems to notice the tell-tale heat in her cheeks, Beth shrugged. 'You'll have to speak to her sooner or later. We're all going to be travelling together. Why not break the ice now? She might be a bit reserved to start with, but I think that's just shyness. She's got a super sense of humour, and she's certainly no dumb blonde.'

Rob's expression had changed several times as she spoke and was now rather baffled. 'You're not jealous?'

Beth kept her face straight. 'Over you?' she enquired, drily.

He flushed again and groaned. 'I didn't mean it *that* way, honestly.'

Lifting one shoulder, Beth sighed softly. 'I'd be a liar if I said there's nothing about myself I'd like to change.' My heart, for example, she thought. I'd trade it for a brand new one of bright shiny stainless steel, untouched and unbreakable.

She glanced over her shoulder at Gaynor who had pulled her chair round to face her mother. From her gestures and expressions Beth guessed she was relating the saga of the repacking. While her mother listened, with an amused smile playing round her mouth, Eugene, revealing mild impatience, took a long swallow from a half-full glass of amber liquid. She heard ice-cubes tinkle. 'But no,' she said, 'I'm not jealous.'

'Hey there,' Eugene raised his gravelly voice, 'are you two all packed ready to go? I'm told we're off pretty early in the morning. Let me get you both a drink.'

Lucille and Gaynor both glanced up and Beth muttered, 'Go on, now's your chance.' Then in her normal voice she said, 'Nothing for me, thanks. I'm all set, except for cleaning and checking my cameras. I'll be doing that after we've eaten. Speaking of which, as I'm supposed to be earning my keep by helping Hofi with the cooking, I'd better start now. Will you excuse me?'

'Sure,' Eugene waved her away, 'you go do whatever you have to.' He turned to Rob. 'How about you, son?'

Beth glanced back as she left the room and saw Rob leaning forward with a dazzling smile that managed to combine both bravado and uncertainty as he shook hands with the still-seated Gaynor.

The kitchen was large and, though it contained all the labour-saving devices, the antique pine wall cupboards and units and an easy-to-clean floor covering in tones of red and brown produced an atmosphere of warmth and cosiness.

The huge pine table was set for eight. Red napkins added a splash of colour alongside gleaming cutlery and glassware.

Beneath the wall cupboards, from the double sink to the fridge-freezer just inside the door to the living-room, the work-top was covered with bowls and dishes. Green salad, potato salad dressed with sour cream and sprinkled with chopped chives, and pickled cucumbers, stood next to plates of feather-light pastries, a chocolate gâteau and a cheesecake.

On the stove a huge pan simmered gently, emitting a delicious savoury aroma.

Hofi stood at the sink, washing up utensils she had used preparing the meal.

'Hofi, I'm starving,' Beth groaned. 'What are we having?'

Hofi jerked round, clearly startled.

'I'm sorry,' Beth apologised at once, concerned by her friend's pallor. 'I thought you had heard me come in. Is there anything I can do?'

Wiping a hand that trembled slightly on the spotless white apron covering her sweater and trousers from chin to knee, Hofi pushed a wisp of hair out of her eyes. 'It's OK.'

She tried to smile. 'My mind was . . . ' She shook her head then glanced at her watch. 'I should be thinking about what I am doing. Now, you wish to help.' She looked around the kitchen, a distracted frown drawing her fair brows together.

Beth moved towards her. 'Hofi, are you all right?'

'Yes, of course,' Hofi replied brightly, not quite meeting Beth's eyes. 'Everything is ready for our meal. As we have American guests, I thought I would not serve too many Icelandic dishes. I have made chicken soup.' She indicated the simmering pan. 'We will have the cold meat on our journey tomorrow. For the main course there is *hangikjot*, you remember our national delicacy, Beth?' Her smile seemed natural for the first time since Beth had entered the kitchen.

Recalling the mouth-watering flavour of the brine-soaked smoked mutton, Beth grimaced and pressed her hands to her midriff. 'Hofi, you're torturing me. My stomach thinks my throat has been cut.'

'Or there is salt herring with various salads and,' she pointed to the work-top, 'a choice of dessert.' Hofi paused at the sound of a vehicle drawing closer. As it stopped and the engine was turned off, she turned to Beth, her cheeks flushed, her eyes suddenly sparkling as she untied her apron. 'Gunnar is here. I will call the others to the table.'

'I'll do that if you like,' Beth offered.

'No,' Hofi said quickly, then immediately tried to soften the sharpness of her refusal. 'I must be a proper hostess and spend a few moments with them. I have been so busy, there has been no time.'

'I'm sure they understand,' Beth said. 'Especially as you're responsible for all the expediton food as well.'

'Even so, it is necessary to do these things properly. If you really want to help, will you warm the soup bowls? And the salads could be put on the table, also the bread rolls. They are in the bin. You do not mind?'

Hofi seemed oddly nervous and Beth was surprised. Surely after organising and catering for tourist and scientific groups for the number of years Hofi had, she should be able to do it blindfold with one arm tied behind her back. Still, as Beth well knew, everyone had their off-days.

'Of course not,' she laughed. 'Go and be a good hostess. This won't take a minute.' She went to the huge dresser, and opening the glass door took down eight bowls. But as she turned to the table, she hesitated. 'Hofi, why eight? There are three Brennans, Rob makes four, then you, me and Gunnar, that's a total of——'

Before Hofi could answer the back door opened and a blond giant lumbered in, his large frame made even bulkier by the parka hanging open over his shirt. With curly golden hair and a full beard, he resembled a Viking from the old Norse legends.

'Beth,' he roared, his face lighting up with welcome, and clasped her in a bear-hug that squeezed all the breath from her body. 'It is good to see you again.'

'It's marvellous to be here, Gunnar,' Beth gasped as he released her, feeling as though her ribs had been crushed.

'You are pleased then with the news?' Gunnar's accent was thicker than Hofi's and his English less fluent. He took off his parka, hanging it on one of the hooks beside the back door.

Hofi tucked her arm through his and immediately he laid his hand over hers and, lowering his head, brushed her temple with his lips. Standing well over six feet, the Icelander made his Junoesque wife look almost petite.

Though Beth was used to the open affection between the two of them, it still touched her, at the same time tearing at her heart like talons, forcing her to recognise an emptiness in her own busy life she steadfastly refused to acknowledge. It rekindled the sense of loss she could not quite banish, even though common sense told her she was better off without Allan. No one as heartless and cynical as he should be grieved over. And she didn't, not any more. Not for a long time.

'I'm absolutely delighted,' Beth grinned at him over her shoulder as she rinsed out the washing-up bowl then filled the sink with hot water in which to warm the soup dishes.

Gunnar looked taken aback. 'You are? I thought maybe——'

'Of course she is pleased,' Hofi interrupted, smiling brightly at her husband as she tugged him towards the living-room door. 'On this expedition, Beth will take many rare and beautiful photographs. She will make much money from them, and win prizes and become very famous. Now, Gunnar, you must come and meet our guests.' She was pulling hard on his arm and Gunnar seemed baffled.

Then he frowned. He asked Hofi a question in their own language and at her brief, hesitant answer, his frown deepened. But before he could voice the protest which was all too clearly hovering on the tip of his tongue, Hofi, talking swiftly, evidently explaining something, drew him out of the kitchen. She smiled reassuringly at Beth as the door closed on the two of them.

Testing the temperature of the bowls and deciding to leave them a moment longer, Beth put the bread rolls intotwo shallow, circular baskets and placed them on the table. Then, after transferring the salads, she returned to the sink.

As she began to dry the bowls she heard footsteps outside. She glanced uncertainly towards the living-room door, wondering if she should call Hofi or Gunnar. She spoke very little Icelandic and if the visitor was the neighbouring farmer whose tractor engine Gunnar was frequently called upon to nurse into relucant life, Beth knew he spoke no English.

Beth quickly began drying the last of the bowls. The expected knock never came. Instead the door opened and a tall man strode in, his thick dark hair looking as if he had run impatient hands through it once too often.

A bulging rucksack was slung over one shoulder and he carried heavy walking-boots, a parka, and rolled waterproofs. Beneath a navy sweater and cords, the heavily muscled shoulders and long, powerful legs indicated a life-style of demanding physical activity.

Beth gave a shaken gasp and, as the newcomer swung round, the bowl slid from her nerveless fingers and shattered on the floor.

For an instant his features registered total astonishment and it was clear that he was as shocked as she by the unexpected encounter.

But within a fraction of a second he had regained control, his lean, hard features tightening, his blue-grey eyes as cold and opaque as arctic ice.

'What the hell are you doing here?' he demanded harshly.

It was two years since she had heard his voice, and yet it was as familiar as her own. But never before had it contained such raw, bitter anger. It sent chills down her spine.

Dropping the cloth on to the work-top, Beth bent down and began picking up the pieces of broken pottery. Her mouth was dry and her legs felt weak. Blood pounded in her ears and her heart beat painfully against her ribs.

Her mind raced. Odd, half-noticed things began clicking into place like tumblers in a combination lock. Hofi's nervousness and distraction, her reluctance to answer questions and her haste in steering the conversation away from details concering the expedition. *Eight places at the table.* Hofi had known Allan was coming. But had she deliberately engineered this meeting? Or had it been genuine coincidence that had brought Allan and herself here at the same time, and Hofi had simply kept quiet, not warning either of them.

'Well?' The single impatient word held not only anger,

but a numbing scorn.

Beth straightened slowly, holding the shards in both hands. There was a faint buzzing in her head. She moistened her lips. 'I—I thought you were in Alaska,' she said dazedly.

'As you can see, I'm not.' He was brusque. 'My work there is finished.' Obviously, this was no fleeting visit then. 'You still haven't told me what you're doing here.'

Beth dropped the broken pieces into the pedal bin and went to the dresser to fetch another bowl. 'In Iceland, or in this house?'

'Both,' he snapped.

Keeping her back to him, Beth rinsed the bowl under the hot tap. Her fingers trembled but she managed, somehow, to hold her voice steady. 'I've been working in the south for a week. Hofi and Gunnar invited me up for a few days' holiday before I fly back to England.' How insistent Hofi had been, pressing her when she demurred, saying how much they had missed her and how they wanted to see for themselves if she had recovered as completely as she claimed. Now she knew why.

She dried the bowl with extra care. 'What about you? May I ask why you're here?' Intuition told her there could be only one reason, and it was nothing to do with her, his shock had been almost as great as her own. But she would not, could not accept it until she had heard it from his own lips.

'I've been called in as a consultant for the Grímsvötn project.'

Beth swallowed. 'On the Vatnajökull glacier?' Her voice sounded quite alien to her.

His eyes narrowed. 'You know about that?'

She nodded briefly. 'Hofi was telling me about it. She didn't mention you.'

Allan was silent, digesting the various implications of her last remark.

Beth couldn't stand it. She had to know for certain. 'You're leading the expedition.' She made it a statement rather than a question.

'Yes.' Allan allowed the rucksack to slide from his shoulders, and placed the parka and waterproofs on top of it in the corner beside the back door. The sound of laughter and conversation drifted in from the living-room.

'What time is your plane?' He threw the question at her.

Beth was confused. 'What plane?'

'The plane taking you back to London,' he replied with exaggerated patience, and started towards her.

Beth backed away, bumping against the work-top, hot colour flooding her cheeks as he stopped at the sink, turned on the tap and began washing his hands. His brief, withering glance told her he had not missed her recoil.

'I—I don't know,' she stammered, furious with herself for allowing him to see how deeply his unexpected arrival had affected her.

'Leaving it a little late, aren't you?' He dried his hands, and turned away to replace the towel on the rail.

'I don't think so,' she retorted, her chin lifting. 'As I'm not returning to England for at least another week, I have plenty of time.' He whirled round, his features darkening, and Beth knew a savage satisfaction at his momentary bewilderment. 'I only arrived today,' she added evenly.

'But—you can't remain here alone.'

'Hofi doesn't intend I should,' Beth said calmly. 'Eugene Brennan has accepted me on the expedition as assistant cook and official photographer.'

It was almost worth the pain, as memories of their first meeting flooded back, to see the shock in his eyes. He remembered too.

His features were rigidly controlled but in his strong neck, the muscles worked. 'No,' he said finally. 'I will not permit it.'

Until that moment, Beth had abandoned the idea of going on the expedition. The sooner she was out of Iceland and away from Allan the sooner she could resume the task of wiping every trace of him from her mind. This meeting, so unexpected, so *shocking*, had been a setback, but she would recover.

Yet to leave now would be clear proof that he still had some power over her, even if it was only the power to make her run.

But wasn't that preferable to remaining where she was obviously not wanted. *Not wanted by whom?*

Whatever her reasons, Hofi had clearly gone to some lengths to ensure her inclusion on the expedition. Gunnar's welcome had been genuinely warm, and he clearly expected her to go with them. All three Brennans, and Rob too, had, in their different ways, made it plain she was as much a part of it as they.

Professionally, it was the break she had been waiting and hoping for. The chance to photograph two immense forces of nature, volcano and glacier, side by side, a phenomenon few people were privileged to see, had been handed to her on a plate. Was she going to toss that chance aside without a second thought?

She remembered something her father had told her as a child. 'Remember, Beth, opportunity often presents itself disguised as a beggar. Turn it away, and it may never knock at your door again.'

Beth's spine straightened and she resolutely ignored the warnings clamouring in her brain. 'I don't think you are in a position to do anything about it.' She kept all the antagonism out of her voice. She wasn't looking for a fight, only recognition that she had as much right as he to be there.

Their gazes clashed and it took all Beth's strength and will-power not to lower hers.

'As you wish,' he said, quietly.

Beth shivered, her victory dust in her mouth. For he had conceded nothing. It was all there in his cold, implacable stare. She had made her choice. The consequences were entirely her responsibility.

The living-room door opened and Gunnar led the party into the kitchen. His questioning glance swept over Beth and Allan and what he saw apparently satisfied him, for he nodded briefly. As he passed Beth on his way to the sink, he murmured, 'You are all right?'

Beth shot him a wry grimace, muttering, 'You don't see any blood, do you?'

But, when his handsome face furrowed in uncertainty, she hastened to reassure him. 'I'm fine, Gunnar. Surprised, I must admit, but OK.'

'My Hofi, she mean well for you, for both of you,' he murmured, his voice a low rumble.

Beth patted his brawny arm. Wasn't there an old saying about the road to hell being paved with good intentions? *My* hell, *Hofi's* intentions, Beth thought, and sighed. 'I know, Gunnar.' She turned, searching for Hofi who had deliberately hung back and was talking with almost feverish animation to Lucille. Rob was making valiant efforts to impress Gaynor who seemed bemused by his non-stop chatter.

'Allan!' Eugene pushed through to pump the younger man's hand. 'Good to see you again. I'd have given just about anything to have seen that burst on the Hubbard.'

'It certainly was something.' Allan grinned down at him, the smile softening the hard planes of his face and making him look suddenly much younger. 'I took some photographs. I've got them with me if you'd like to see them later.'

'*Would I?*' Eugene beamed. 'Now listen, you folks.' He turned to face them, raising one hand in a bid for silence.

As everyone looked round, Beth caught Hofi's anxious glance and rolled her eyes, letting her friend know that all was still well between them. A great wave of relief crossed Hofi's face and her shoulders visibly sagged as though a weight had been lifted from them.

'No speeches now, Eugene,' Lucille warned. 'We're in here to eat, the talking can wait.'

'Hush, woman,' her husband growled. 'All I want to say is this. We are privileged to have leading us on this trip one of the most knowledgeable and experienced men in glaciology,' his mouth quirked in mock-disgust, 'even if he is only a youngster.'

'Hardly a youngster,' Allan demurred, pointing to the sprinkling of silver hairs at his temple. Which Beth hadn't noticed until now. But strangely, it did not make him look older, conferring instead an authority which sat easily on his broad shoulders.

He is thirty-four, Beth thought. Thirty-four years, six months and two weeks old.

'Anyhow,' Eugene announced, 'I intend to learn as much as he can teach me between here and our destination, and I'd advise the rest of you to do the same. There won't be another opportunity like this. Now, I guess I'd better introduce you around here. Look like you already met Mizz Farrell.'

As Allan's gaze flickered towards her, his dark brows lifting fractionally at the name, Beth's chin rose. What small success she could claim was entirely due to her own efforts. Using his name would doubtless have smoothed her path but—she fought the spasm of bitter pain—it had not *legally* been hers to use. She was her own woman now, totally independent.

'Yes,' Allan said quietly, 'Miss Farrell and I have introduced ourselves.'

'Beth's a photographer,' Eugene rattled on, 'a good one,

so she tells me. I'm relying on her to keep a visual record of this expedition. There has been mention of her helping our hostess here with the cooking, but I don't know how much time she'll have for that. See here, Beth,' he turned sharp eyes on her, 'if it comes to a choice, you make sure you got a camera in your hands. We can eat any time, but the films you take here will be irreplaceable. You hear me?'

'Loud and clear, Eugene,' Beth grinned at him.

'Right. Now, this here's my wife, Lucille.' He put a fond arm around her plump shoulders. 'She was away visiting her sister in Vermont last time you were in the States, Allan, that's how you missed her. She catalogues all my specimens for me and does bird paintings. We got walls full of 'em back home. She's got a real deft hand.'

Allan shook hands with Lucille who couldn't resist a quick glance at her daughter and, Beth realised with an odd wrenching sensation, was speculating on the possibilities of a match even as she dimpled under his friendly smile.

'And this here's my daughter, Gaynor. She don't do much of anything 'cept spend money. But then, what else is a pretty girl for?' He laughed, clearly oblivious to the stark pain in Gaynor's lovely eyes as she forced a smile and offered Allan her hand.

'How do you do, Dr Bryce.' Beth saw Allan's gaze suddenly sharpen at the quiet dignity in the girl's husky voice. 'I hope I can be of use rather than just a passenger on this trip. Perhaps if Beth is too busy, I can take her place with the cooking.'

Eugene snorted. 'What do you know about anything like that? Hell, you can't even——'

'I should be most grateful for Gaynor's help, Mr Brennan—Eugene,' Hofi said quickly. 'There is much that she can do.'

Eugene opened his mouth and took a breath, but Lucille nudged him hard, so he closed it again and shrugged.

'I never carry passengers,' Allan said softly. He was still holding Gaynor's hand and, as she looked up at him, her slow smile of gratitude made her radiant.

Beth inadvertently caught Rob's eye, and he shot her a wry, hopeless grin.

'Please, let us sit now,' Hofi said, 'and I will serve the meal.'

As everyone found a seat, Eugene introduced Rob to Allan who, within seconds, had drawn from the rather startled young man all the relevant details concerning his background, schooling, university course and degree, his specialisation and practical experience.

Seated between Hofi and Rob who had Gaynor on his other side, Beth forced down her soup. Her appetite had vanished and her stomach was a small, tight knot.

'You are not too angry with me?' Hofi whispered as Beth helped her carry the dirty soup bowls to the sink.

'Did you plan it, Hofi?' Beth murmured back.

'I?' Hofi snorted. 'I wish I had such power. It was fate, Beth, I swear to you. Allan wrote telling of his appointment to the Grímsvötn project and his agreement to lead Eugene's expedition. It seems he and Eugene have been friends for some years . . . ' Just one more thing I didn't know, Beth thought. ' . . . I think they met when Allan was doing one of his lecture tours for the Geographical Society. The point is that Allan does not have to be on the glacier for several days and Eugene desperately wanted the chance to see Vatnajökull for himself. So he offered to put up the funds if Allan would head a properly organised expedition to observe as many as possible of the country's geological features. The dates were agreed with us, then you phoned and—well—' She shrugged helplessly. 'Beth, it is wrong that you two should be apart.'

'Hofi,' Beth gritted, 'we had no right to be together.'

Clattering the dishes in her agitation, Hofi hissed, 'That

is ridiculous. If ever two people were meant for each other, it is you and Allan. Even Gunnar says so. When we met you on your honeymoon, he told me you were the most well suited couple he had ever seen except us. What are you talking about, *no right*? I do not understand. You do not make sense.'

The lump in Beth's throat threatened to choke her. What could she say? She had told no one, not even her mother, the real reason she had left Allan. Saying as little as possible, she had, when pressed, made terse reference to irreconcilable differences, then devoted all her energies to expunging him from her memory . . . *and failed.*

'Hofi,' Gunnar's patient, rumbling voice rose above the general murmur of conversation. 'You sit us down to feed us, so where is the food?'

'Coming, coming.' As Hofi went to the fridge to fetch the salt herring and a large platter of sliced smoked mutton, Beth slipped back into her chair, only too aware of Allan's probing gaze and the pricking of her eyelids.

After the meal, she hurried upstairs, hoping for a few moments' solitude in which to collect herself. But Gaynor came up right behind her to repair her lipstick and flick a comb through the already perfect hair. She was glowing with happiness and kept saying how kind everyone was to make her so welcome.

With no possibility of feigning a headache or any other minor indisposition, Beth had little choice but to pick up her camera case and follow a still chattering Gaynor downstairs once more.

CHAPTER THREE

'No two glaciers are alike,' Allan was saying as Beth moved quietly to an armchair set slightly to one side of the group formed by the others.

She laid her case flat on the floor by her feet and, taking her 35 millimetre Nikon, now empty of film, began to dismantle and clean it.

'Each has its own pattern of growth, or shrinkage,' Allan continued, acknowledging with a brief smile Gaynor's apology as she settled herself gracefully into the only space available, which was between her mother and Rob. He ignored Beth. 'But even that can be unpredictable. A glacier can create its own weather system. It is constantly moving, flowing like a vast, slow-motion river. Its normal rate of advance may be only a few inches a year then, for reasons we do not yet fully understand, it will suddenly surge.'

'Like the Hubbard?' Eugene interjected.

Allan nodded. 'At one point, a tributary glacier of the Hubbard was moving forward one hundred and thirty feet *a day* . Like all rivers the centre moves faster than the edges, which are restrained by friction against the sides of the valley down which it's flowing. But this isn't water we're talking about, it's millions of tons of ice up to one thousand feet thick tearing up massive boulders and gouging out the valley sides as it gallops downhill. Nor is it a solid sheet. There are numerous cracks and meltwater tunnels running through it, and the surface moves faster than the base. The pressures and stresses within the ice rip it apart, splitting it into huge fissures and crevasses hundreds of feet deep.'

He had them spellbound, Beth realised. Even her own hands had fallen still and instinctively she had raised her head to watch him as he talked, listening not only to what he was saying, but to the rise and fall of his voice, its pitch and resonance stirring yet more memories.

Quickly lowering her eyes, she concentrated on the open camera, using a soft brush and fine cloth to remove every speck of dust.

It was hardly surprising he was in such demand for lectures and seminars. He loved his work and, despite preferring to be out in the field pursuing the practical side of it, he had a rare gift for communicating this passionate interest to audiences.

Illustrating his talks with slides, he drew them into his world, painting word pictures, relating frightening or amusing incidents, so that those listening felt they had actually been there, standing beneath towering ice-cliffs glistening blue-white or pale green in the sunshine, hearing the rending groan and explosive crash as new icebergs were calved, feeling fog's clammy fingers brush their skin as they smelled the dankness of a looming berg on a flat-calm sea.

With heart-wrenching clarity Beth remembered slipping into one of those lectures. He had been speaking in London ten months after they had parted. The lectures had been widely advertised and she had been so confident, quite convinced her anger had cleansed her of all feeling for him. She had decided to go simply as a test, certain that she would be able to view the slides and listen to his commentary with total objectivity.

She had sneaked out before the lights went up so that no one would notice and wonder at her tears.

Eugene leafed through the glossy seven-by-eleven-inch photographs Allan had passed him, and his lips pursed in a soundless whistle.

All the others hunched forward to look, pointing and exclaiming.

Beth glanced up to find Allan watching her, a cold smile
at the corners of his mouth. His narrowed eyes glittered. He
raised one dark brow. Beth recognised the challenge. He
didn't care whether she looked at the photographs or not.
But, *if* she didn't someone was sure to ask why. He was
waiting to see what she would do.

The situation was taken out of her hands by Eugene, who
thrust the prints at her. 'What do you think of these then,
girl?'

Laying her camera down, Beth took the prints and
examined them carefully. There was an air of expectancy as
everyone waited for her reply.

Eugene had placed her in an impossible position, though
of course he didn't realise it. If she did what everyone
anticipated, and said they were wonderful, which in terms
of subject matter they were, she would be compromising
her professional integrity. She would also sacrifice her self-
respect.

Feeling Allan's gaze upon her, she raised her eyes. The
tension was immediate, electric, an invisible charge
between them. For an instant it was as though they were
alone in the room. She saw his eyes widen fractionally,
then, like steel doors slamming, they were suddenly blank,
opaque, revealing nothing.

She looked squarely at Eugene, her heart still thudding
from the jolt. 'As far as content is concerned, I should think
they're unique.' There was a general murmur of agreement.

'*But?*' Allan said, so softly that only she heard him. She
took a breath.

'But technically——' a sudden silence fell '—and I intend
no disrespect to Dr Bryce,' Beth swallowed, 'they are
clearly the work of an amateur rather than a professional.'
She could only tell the truth. If he chose to interpret it as a
sniper's attack, there was nothing she could do.

She was aware of glances swivelling between Allan and

herself, of curiosity and mild unease, of bewilderment and
hesitancy.

'Would you care to elaborate?' Allan suggested pleasantly
and Beth felt ice-water trickle down her spine.

'Yeah, what d'ya mean?' Eugene frowned. 'They look
pretty damn good to me.'

Beth selected one and turned it outwards to face him.
'This tumbling wall of ice is an incredible sight. It's
awesome and terrifying. But without a human figure in the
picture we get no sense of *how* huge it is. It could be twenty
feet high, or two hundred.' She didn't wait for reaction, but
hurried on. 'Dr Bryce has chosen his angle well, we can see
a little of the grassy bank on which he's standing. But if he
had stood even further back and had one of his colleagues
somewhere near the centre of the picture, preferably
wearing an orange or yellow waterproof for colour contrast
against the grass and the ice, he would have had a far better-
balanced photograph with even greater impact as to the
scale and power of the glacier.'

Allan stretched out his hand. Beth passed the photograph
to him and he studied it, frowning. To Beth his silence
seemed to last an eternity. The others started talking
amongst themselves.

'You're quite right,' he said at last and as he looked up
she read both surprise and respect in his gaze.

Carefully, so that no one would notice, Beth released the
breath she hadn't been aware of holding.

'Well, looks like you know what you're talking about,
girl,' Eugene grudgingly admitted, and Beth bit her tongue,
knowing he didn't realise how patronising he sounded.
'That's the kind of stuff I want to take back to Texas with
me. Can you do that?'

'I can't promise you a glacier surge,' Beth said wryly, 'but
you'll get the best work I can do.'

'Your folio, Beth,' Hofi said suddenly. 'You always carry it with you. Please bring it down. When Eugene has seen it he will have no more doubts, *or* questions. I will make coffee for us all.'

When Beth hesitated, Gaynor rose from the sofa. 'Let me fetch it.' She smiled at Beth. 'After all your help, it's the least I can do.'

Beth was torn. The photographs in the folio were intensely personal to her, a collection built up mostly over the past two years, each one reflecting a mood, capturing the essence of an emotion. Each one a little piece of her soul.

Yet Hofi was right, they would silence all doubts as to her professional expertise. Allan's sudden reappearance in her life had cracked her shell of self-assurance and exposed her commitment to solitude as a hollow sham. She was vulnerable and uncertain. She needed a rock to cling to until the turmoil within her subsided and she was once more in total control. Her work was that rock, the safe harbour into which she could retreat and shut out a world she couldn't cope with.

'How much persuasion do you need to show us these masterpieces?' Rob pleaded. 'You want blood? My back teeth? I'm sing you the Hallelujah Chorus if you like.'

Beth gave in at once. She had no patience with false modesty and did not want to gain a reputation for resorting to such ego-boosting tactics. Not knowing the true situation, none of them understood the reason for her reluctance.

'You've persuaded me,' she said quickly to Rob, who grinned.

'It always works. The Hallelujah Chorus swings it. I haven't had to sing it yet.'

Beth turned to Gaynor. 'It's a brown leather zip-up folder strapped to the inside of the lid of my suitcase.'

Gaynor hurried off upstairs, Hofi went out to the kitchen

and Allan joined Eugene and Gunnar in a discussion about the planned route and various hazards they might encounter.

Beth reassembled the first camera and began cleaning the second. A shadow fell across her hands and she glanced up to see Rob watching her. She grinned at him and carried on working.

He squatted beside her. 'You were right,' he murmured.

'What about?' Deftly, Beth screwed a macro lens on to the Olympus camera, ready for close-ups of lava-formation or flowers, and gave it a final careful polish.

'Gaynor. She's not at all like I imagined.'

'Women rarely are,' Beth murmured with wistful irony.

'But I don't seem to be making much headway.' He laughed, a little too off-hand.

'Oh, Rob,' Beth said softly, with quick understanding. 'So soon?'

He nodded, his grin lop-sided, shaky. 'Ridiculous, isn't it? I hardly know her. But she's the one, Beth.'

Beth stayed silent, realising he was sorting out his own thoughts, as much as talking to her.

'Only how do I get her to see it the same way? She's friendly but too polite. There's a distance, as though she's deliberately keeping a space between herself and the rest of us—well, me, anyway.'

Beth debated with herself for a moment, then made a decision. After all, Eugene and Lucille had made no secret of it.

'She's only twenty-five, Rob, and she's been through two divorces. Gaynor is no hard-as-nails rich bitch.' Beth recalled with a pang of shame her own instant judgement of the lovely blonde. 'I think she feels she's a failure. She's also been badly hurt. It's hardly surprising she's not ready to rush into another relationship. Perhaps if you give her a little time, don't crowd or rush her. Perhaps you could let *her* talk once in a while?' Beth glanced sideways at him, her sympathetic smile taking the sting out of her suggestion.

He grimaced. 'That noticeable, was it?'

Beth nodded. 'She was beginning to look a little glazed at dinner.'

Rob shrugged, suddenly despairing. 'I don't know why I'm bothering, except I can't help myself. I mean, it's pretty obvious she's not really interested. Oh, she's pleasant to me. But with competition like that,' he jerked his head, 'what chance have I got?'

Beth was still. 'What competition? What are you talking about?'

'Him,' Rob muttered. 'Dr Allan Bryce.'

No. Beth flinched at the swift, vicious jab of pain.

'And do you know what's worse?' Rob went on, oblivious to the battle raging within Beth.

'No,' she managed. *It didn't matter to her, Allan could do what he liked with whomever he wanted. She didn't care.*

'No one could help admiring the man. But, damn it, I *like* him as well.'

Beth quietly cleared the choking obstruction from her throat. 'I think you're imagining it.'

Rob shook his head. 'I wish I were.'

'Come on,' Beth tried to rally him, crushing her own rising sense of desperation. 'Faint heart never won fair lady. Anyway, it takes two, and I don't think he's shown Gaynor any special attention.'

'That's because you haven't been watching. I have,' Rob said dismally. 'I know what I've seen and it doesn't inspire me with hope for *my* cause.'

'I—I don't know what to suggest,' Beth stammered.

'Why should you?' Rob made a brave effort at a smile. 'It's not your problem, is it? Ah, coffee, thank God.'

Hofi placed the tray on a side table and began setting out the cups and saucers. Gaynor returned with the folio. Rob stood up, his eyes betraying him as he watched her hand it to Beth.

'Did you have to go to school to learn how to do it?' Gaynor asked shyly.

Beth nodded, and, opening the case out, touched the collection of photographs gently with her fingertips, drawing strength and confidence from them.

'I did a two-year diploma course at a College of Art and Design. We learned about different types of cameras and lenses, and their uses, black and white and colour printing, how to made videos and movies for the cinema, and about different kinds of lighting.'

But Gaynor had stopped listening. Craning her neck, she was gazing, wide-eyed, at the jumble of prints of various sizes. 'Oh, Beth,' she breathed, 'they're—fabulous. Look, Rob.' She turned, beckoning him forward as she held up a print taken from a hillside at dawn, a study in violet, pale mauve and lilac with mist lying like a thick silver quilt in the valley below. 'Isn't that just beautiful?

'It certainly is,' he agreed softly, then turned his head to look at the photograph.

'Hofi?' Beth heard Gunnar's voice above the quiet babble of conversation.

'I must—I'll be back in a moment.' Hofi pressed his arm. 'Beth will you pour the coffee for me?'

'Of course.' Handing the folder to Gaynor and Rob, who had settled themselves on the carpet, Beth jumped up from her chair.

To reach the table she had to pass Allan who appeared to be deep in conversation with Eugene. He must have heard the exchange, but made no attempt to step either forwards or back out of her way. Other than going all the way round the back of the semicircle of chairs and sofas, she had no choice but to brush against him as she squeezed past with a muttered, 'Excuse me.'

She knew by the ironic lift of his dark brows that he had seen the tide of colour flush her face, but his conversation with Eugene never faltered.

She wished fiercely she had trodden on his toes, hard.

The photographs were being passed on now. They had reached Lucille and Gunnar. Eugene would be next. Then Allan. Beth's hand shook momentarily. Would he see beyond the image on the surface?

Beth deliberately blanked her mind. Speculating about Allan Bryce's thoughts and reactions was a total waste of time. In any case, they were not the least bit important to her.

She handed Gaynor and Lucille their coffee, offering cream and sugar so that they could help themselves. She did the same for each of the men, leaving Allan until last. When she had poured his, automatically leaving it black, and adding one spoonful of sugar, she handed it to him, then picked up the coffee-pot, intending to take it out to the kitchen for a refill.

Something in Allan's voice as he said 'thank you' made her look back. But it was his mocking smile, a smile that held a hint of triumph, as he looked up from his coffee cup, that made her realise what she had done.

Ignoring the betraying heat in her cheeks, she snatched up the cream jug. But before she could offer it to him, he half turned, so that only she could hear him, murmuring, 'And after all this time too. I wonder what else you remember, *Miss Farrell.*' He almost spat her name and Beth flinched.

'*Nothing,*' she hissed, and almost ran to the kitchen, before her draining colour revealed the lie for what it was.

Quickly shutting the kitchen door behind her, she leaned against it, breathing deeply to try and calm her racing heart. Something was very wrong. *She* was the injured party, the innocent victim of his ruthless deceit. Yet he radiated a simmering anger that suggested he blamed *her*.

Beth became aware suddenly that Hofi hadn't moved, hadn't turned to see who had come in even though she must have heard the door open and close. Standing at the sink, her back to Beth as she stared out of the window, Hofi was unnaturally still.

Forcing her own troubles aside, Beth hurried across to her friend. 'Are you all right?'

It was obvious she wasn't. Her face was ashen and tiny drops of sweat beaded her upper lip and forehead.

'Hofi? What is it?' Beth asked anxiously.

Hofi managed a shaky smile. 'Nothing really. I felt a bit——' She could not find the word and instead made a small circling motion above her head with one hand.

'Dizzy?' Beth supplied.

Hofi nodded. 'But I am all right now. Truly, Beth.' She wiped her forehead with the back of her hand. 'I just was waiting for it to pass. I was bending down and I think I stood up too fast.'

Beth was sympathetic. 'I've done that myself. It makes you quite faint for a minute or two. Are you OK now?'

'I'm fine. What did you come in for?'

Beth lifted the metal pot. 'More coffee.'

Hofi's face contorted in an involuntary grimace. 'Please—will you make it? The smell—I cannot——' She shuddered and, reaching into a cupboard, took down a glass and poured herself some water. She sipped slowly at first then, as her colour returned, she drained the glass. 'Now I am perfectly all right.' She smiled at Beth. 'See?' The smile faded to concern. 'What about you?'

Beth turned quickly away, busying herself with the percolator. 'Me? Terrific.'

'No,' Hofi's voice was gentle. 'I mean you and Allan.'

Beth shrugged. 'He calls me Miss Farrell . . . ' With real venom, she remembered and felt goose-pimples erupt on her arms. 'I call him Dr Bryce. As far as everyone else knows we have only just met. It seems to be the most logical way of handling the situation, and saves everyone from embarrassment.'

Hofi looked horrified. 'But you cannot spend the whole expedition in such—such——' She broke into a torrent of Icelandic as the strain on her English proved too great.

Beth switched off the percolator. 'There doesn't seem to be a viable alternative.' She poured the fresh, steaming coffee into the pot. 'Especially as neither of us is prepared to leave the expedition.'

'Then there is hope.' Hofi touched Beth's shoulder. 'You will be together all the week. You will remember all that you shared together, all that you meant to each other——'

'*Don't!*' Beth burst out, her face anguished. 'It's too late, Hofi. Whatever was there is dead, finished.'

Liar, her heart accused.

'I don't believe that,' Hofi said with quiet conviction. 'If it was finished, if it was dead as you say, you would not be hurting like this. Allan is part of you, Beth. He is in your blood.' Her face softened. 'He adored you. He would watch you when you did not know, and all that was inside him, all the love and tenderness, was on his face. It would shine from his eyes.' She shook her head. 'I could not believe it when you told me you had parted. It made no sense. I could never understand what could have . . . ' She spread her hands in a gesture of complete bewilderment. 'I never asked before, perhaps it is wrong I ask now . . . '

Beth knew what was coming, and for the first time she did not shy away. She wanted, no *needed*, to tell someone, and Hofi was her closest friend.

'What happened, Beth? What went wrong between you?'

Beth's throat was stiff and sore with unshed tears. The coffee-pot forgotten, her eyes were wide, blank, as she relived for the millionth time that terrible moment when, in response to frantic hammering, she had opened the door of Allan's flat. Shalana had stood on the threshold, and within seconds Beth's world had shattered into fragments.

She jerked round. She would not cry. She had cried too long and too hard over the past twenty-four months. Her voice was harsh, painful. 'He was everything I had ever dreamed of. Our lives were full and happy. We had our work and we had each other. There was just one small thing he had forgotten to tell me.' Beth picked up the coffee-pot. 'He already had a wife.'

Leaving Hofi staring, open-mouthed and speechless, after her, Beth went back into the living-room.

Her photographs were on every lap and as she walked in, Gaynor was the first to look up openly, admiring. 'Beth, you are one very talented lady. I'm hoping some of it might rub off on me. I won't get in your way,' she added quickly. 'I brought my own camera along. It's one of those that practically takes pictures by itself. You know, you just point it and press the button. Do you think it'll be all right?'

Beth felt a little of her tension ease away. It was impossible not to like Gaynor. 'If it's as "all right" as your jacket, it will be fine. Can you remember what make it is?'

Gaynor's forehead puckered as she thought hard. 'Hass . . . Hassel—something. I think.'

Beth nodded. 'Hasselblad.' She might have known. Gaynor possessed one of the most expensive small cameras in existence, a camera many professionals, including Beth, would give their right arms for, and to her it was just another toy. 'You'll get by with that,' she said, unable to suppress the gentle irony.

She moved around the room, refilling coffee cups, answering questions about shutter-speeds, filters, lenses, the brand of film she favoured, and the locations.

By keeping herself busy it was easy to avoid Allan, but some sixth sense told her each time his cold gaze turned her way. Then the hair on the back of her neck began to prickle and she knew he was approaching. She set the coffee-pot back on the tray. If she could not quite hide the tremor in her hands, she had no intention of advertising it.

She turned to face him, her chin lifting. Defiant, vulnerable, she was poised to fight, to defend herself. For though his expression was bland, she sensed an aura around him, an air of threat that filled her with foreboding and made her heart pump harder, faster.

He raised the sheaf of photographs. 'I wish I could say Gaynor Brennan doesn't know what she's talking about, that these are just corny, sentimental junk,' he paused, his gaze impaling her like a cold steel blade, 'but I can't. You may be a first-class bitch, and a cheat, and a coward, *Miss Farrell*, but you have a rare gift for photography.' He thrust the prints into her hands.

Beth's mouth was dry with shock. 'H—How *d-dare* you . . . ' She could hardly get the words out.

His mouth twisted. 'Oh, it's no problem. I just remember what you did. After that,' he shrugged, 'it's easy.'

Beth cringed under the look of disgust on his face as he turned away, as if unable to stand the sight of her any longer.

What *she* had done? What *had* she done but walk away from a man who had married her knowing he was already married to somebody else, that their 'marriage' was a mockery, a pretence, a total lie? What else *could* she have done?

Her chest hurt as she struggled to suppress a sob. He had no right to accuse her, *he* was the guilty one. Biting the inside of her lip so hard she tasted blood, Beth lowered her head and blinked the tears away. She had been the fool.

Allan raised his hands. 'Your attention, everybody.'

All conversation stopped as heads turned towards him.

'I think it would be a fitting start, a signal that our expedition is officially under way, if we all step outside for a

moment and have a group photograph taken against the
midnight sun.'

A chorus of approval greeted his words. Beth heard
Gaynor say delightedly, 'What a romantic idea,' and the
blade pierced a little deeper.

'But, before we go,' Allan continued, 'I want to make a
couple of things clear. First, as leader, my word is law. It
has nothing to do with ego-trips and everything to do with
safety. Second, we will carry no alcohol, not even for
medicinal purposes.' Rob gave a good-natured groan and
Eugene muttered something then, as Lucille dug him in the
ribs and told him his liver could do with the rest, subsided
with a shrug.

'The laws here governing drinking and driving are among
the strictest in Europe. But apart from that, each one of you
must be fit and ready to help with driving at a moment's
notice. This will apply particularly at river crossings, where
we may have to tow the vehicles across ourselves. Now, are
you all prepared to accept these conditions?'

Everyone nodded, and amid the murmuring of 'sure,' and
'yeah, I guesss so,' Allan turned to Beth.

'You still want to come?' he demanded softly, and she
knew he wanted her to back out.

If she stayed he would not misuse his authority, of that
she was certain. He would never compromise the safety of
the expedition, or his professional reputation. But, one way
or another, his eyes, hard and bright as ice-crystals, warned,
he would exact revenge for her defiance.

Gathering her courage, Beth met his gaze. She had come
too far and there was too much at stake both professionally,
and in terms of her painfully rebuilt self-respect, to give up
now. 'Of course I'm coming,' she said as if there had never
been any doubt of it.

His eyes narrowed a fraction more. 'So be it,' he said.

With his words echoing in her mind, Beth ran upstairs

to fetch her tripod and a fresh film, trying to smother the apprehension welling up inside her.

CHAPTER FOUR

As ROB and Eugene passed up the cases, Gunnar and Allan, one on the roof of each vehicle, lashed them securely in place with rope.

The water and diesel cans had been filled and checked, so had the spares. All the food was carefully packed in the mobile kitchen to be towed behind Gunnar's Land Rover, with the exception of their picnic lunch. Hofi was stowing the plastic boxes in netting panniers attached to the back seats.

Gaynor had brushed her hair up into a loose knot, exposing her pale neck and giving her an even more pronounced air of vulnerability. Without make-up she looked fresh-faced and much younger. And yet, with her cream cashmere sweater knotted around her shoulders and the sleeves of her lilac shirt turned back, she still managed to look as if she had just stepped off the cover of a glossy magazine.

Unconsciously, Beth ran one hand through her feathery crop. She rubbed the back of her neck, trying to smooth away the tension, a legacy from her restless night.

Gaynor took a photo of Lucille, who was carrying a thick, folded car rug. 'What d'you want that for, Momma? It's not cold,' Beth heard her ask as she lowered the camera.

'Who said anything about the cold?' Lucille retorted. 'I've been on these trips before. It's the jolting and vibration that kills you. A body my age needs all the comfort and protection it can get.'

Beth moved away and snapped Eugene and Rob with their heads together, Eugene watching as Rob expertly spliced the fraying end of a rope

She moved back further and took what she knew was a really good shot of Gunnar and Allan as they bent over the luggage, silhouetted against the morning sun hanging low in a clear aquamarine sky.

As she lowered the camera Allan straightened up. He stared down at her for a moment but, with the sun behind him, she could not read his expression. Then he turned away. She felt a need to justify herself and wanted to shout, 'This isn't for me, it's for Eugene. It's what I'm being paid for,' and had to bite her tongue, hard.

'Right,' Allan raised his voice, demanding their attention. 'Everybody ready?'

In spite of everything, Beth felt a frisson of excitement and knew it was shared by the others. A chorus of assent floated on the crisp air as Allan jumped down and scooped his sweater up off the grass.

His pale blue knitted sports-shirt clung to his upper body, defining the muscles in his shoulders and back. There wasn't an ounce of spare flesh on him and, though he looked superbly fit, Beth could tell he had lost weight. Even as the realisation surfaced she trampled on it. Making comparisons between now and *then* meant opening the flood-gates to memories, and that was something she could not, dare not, allow.

Hooking the thick webbing strap of her camera around her neck, she quickly bent to fasten the foam-lined aluminium case in which she carried both her cameras and all their accessories. That too had a thick shoulder strap as well as a handle.

Hofi had locked the back door and, with her heavy golden plait falling over her T-shirted shoulder, she came to join Beth. 'You look tired,' she whispered sympathetically. 'Didn't you sleep?'

'You are looking heaps better,' Beth replied with a quick smile, avoiding a direct answer. 'Recovered from your dizzy spell?'

To her surprise Hofi went pink and lowered her eyes. 'It was nothing, I told you.' She looked up anxiously. 'Beth, you did not say anything to anyone else, did you?'

Beth's eyebrows lifted. 'Oh yes. I took out a full-page ad in the local paper.' She sighed. 'Of course I didn't tell anyone. Who would I tell?'

Hofi shot her a quick glance. 'Gunnar.'

'Well, I didn't. You said you were OK, so I—to be honest, Hofi, I forgot all about it.' Her mouth twisted briefly. 'I had rather a lot on my mind.' Concern drew her brows together. 'You are all right, aren't you?'

Hofi squeezed Beth's forearm. 'I promise you, there's nothing wrong with me. '

Beth was struck once more by Hofi's glowing colour and the sparkle in her eyes.

'Gunnar worries for me, that is all,' she added hastily. 'And when he worries, he . . . what is the word?' She wagged her finger, pulled a stern face, and made a repeating gesture.

'Nags?' Beth offered, half joking.

Hofi considered a moment, then nodded, her expression serious. '*Já*, yes. And I do not want nags. So please, you say nothing?'

Nonplussed, Beth shrugged. 'OK.'

With a swift grateful smile, Hofi hurried over to her waiting husband, kissed his bearded cheek, and climbed into the back seat of the lead Land Rover.

Beth sucked in a deep breath. Who would be travelling with whom? She didn't know which vehicle she would prefer to be in. If she rode with Hofi, questions would be unavoidable. She had seen concern and curiosity hovering in her friend's eyes since last evening, and Hofi was clearly anxious to direct attention away from herself.

Yet, the way things were between Allan and herself, riding with him would be even harder. But, as he had made plain, he was in charge, he would decide, and doubtless would have excellent reasons, whatever his choice.

As if reading her mind, Allan swung round. 'You and

Gaynor will ride with me.' Beth merely nodded, but Gaynor's face lit up. Rob couldn't mask his anxiety and Beth looked away from his open relief when Allan continued, 'Rob, you will come with me as well. In the front,' he added smoothly, apparently not noticing Gaynor's disappointment as she clambered into the back.

Eugene helped Lucille get comfortable beside Hofi, then, with an agility that belied his years, jumped up into the front seat next to Gunnar.

Doors slammed, bags and sweaters were stowed. Directly behind Allan, Beth wedged her camera case on the floor between her foot and the doorsill.

There was a loud crackling noice and a distorted voice filled the vehicle.

'Gee, what's that?' Gaynor whispered in alarm.

Rob smiled over his shoulder at her as Allan picked up the hand-mike, pressed the switch and spoke into it.

'Two-way radio. The vehicles can keep in contact with one another and, in the event of an emergency, we can call for help. All mod cons here.'

Then Allan started the engine and, following Gunnar on to the road, they were off.

'Isn't this great?' Smiling widely, her eyes bright with excitement, Gaynor had to shout above the throaty roar of the diesel engine.

Beth nodded and was comforted by the fact that while they were on the move, at least, conversation would be minimal.

Turning her head forward, her vision was immediately filled by Allan's broad shoulders and thick dark hair. It had been recently cut, she noticed, and lay, no longer curling, but neat on his strong neck. Her gaze shifted fractionally and caught him watching her through the rear-view mirror.

She looked away at once, unable to stem the hot tide that flooded her face and throat, and turned her head to look out of the side window.

Cattle grazed in the rich meadows, the lush green grass a vivid contrast to the bare rock of the hillsides on their right and the ruffled blue water on their left as they headed south to the head of the fjord and across the river.

She should not have come. Bravado was all very well, but a moment's defiance was a vastly different proposition from the reality of living twenty-four hours a day for the next week within touching distance of one another. Allan's dislike of her and the constant undercurrent of anger were almost tangible in their strength. Yet Rob and Gaynor seemed not to notice anything amiss.

Maybe they were both too wrapped up in their own thoughts or, could it be that there *wasn't* an atmosphere? That it was all in her overwrought imagination? A product of the shock of seeing Allan again?

Without turning her head, she glanced sideways and their eyes met again. Common sense told her he could not have been driving *and* constantly watching her. Yet he had known the exact moment . . . This time he looked away first. It was deliberate, like a slap.

Beth moved further along the seat, closer to the door, out of his sight-line. She had to twist sideways to avoid her leg pressing on the metal edge of the case. It wasn't comfortable and she knew she couldn't sustain it, but she'd stick it out as long as possible.

Gaynor leaned forward, resting her forearms along the back of each front seat and began talking to both men, her lovely face animated.

Allan answered her, half turning his head. She said something else and broke into soft gurgling laughter. It was a happy sound, infectious, and both men joined in, though Rob sounded a little strained.

Beth's heart went out to him and she continued to stare out of the window, remembering the previous evening.

The party had broken up after coffee and everyone had gone

to their rooms.

Beth had undressed, put on her pyjamas, washed, cleaned her teeth and climbed into bed before Gaynor had even finished removing her make-up.

And Gaynor had wanted to talk. About Allan.

'Isn't he just something else?' she murmured as she slowly brushed her gleaming hair. 'He's got this kinda *magnetism*. Don't you think so, Beth?' She paused, the brush in mid-air, and turned round, clearly expecting an answer.

Beth muttered something non-committal and adjusted her pillows, keeping her head averted.

'Aw, come on,' Gaynor coaxed, 'don't you think he's rather special? God, charisma was invented for him.' She ticked off the points on her fingers. 'He's handsome, he has brains, and charm, and a way of looking into a person's eyes that . . . well, I tell you, Beth, it just makes my knees go weak.'

Beth dredged up her brightest smile and felt hysteria bubbling inside her. *What was she to do?*

Don't fall for him, she wanted to plead. You'll get hurt again. He's married. He was already married when he married me.

She couldn't say that. She couldn't say anything. For Allan had made no attempt to explain to the others that they had known one another before. She was as much to blame, for she too had allowed the impression that they were strangers to stand uncorrected. At the time it had seemed the most sensible thing to do, but already the problems were creeping in.

If she tried to warn Gaynor off, without mentioning her own involvement, Gaynor would immediately assume that she was jealous and wanted Allan for herself. Though, God knew, after what she had suffered, nothing could be further from the truth.

Gaynor would also, quite reasonably, want to know how and where she had obtained her information.

If she admitted it was personal experience, Gaynor might

tackle Allan about it. What if he denied ever meeting her before last night?

He was becoming well-known. Being good-looking and still relatively young, it was not uncommon for women he had barely met to claim a much deeper, more significant relationship. During their time together he and Beth had laughed about it.

But everything was different now. His grey eyes held bitterness and condemnation. He might well accuse her of doing exactly the same thing.

Not only would she look an utter fool, but the atmosphere between Gaynor and herself would be poisoned.

They had to share a tent for a week. There would be tensions enough just coping with the ordinary pressures of the expedition without deliberately adding to them.

So Beth choked it all back. Gaynor would have to find out for herself, just as she had done.

'He's certainly good-looking,' she had managed, elaborately casual. 'I hadn't noticed the charm.' To her he had shown about as much charm as a cobra.

Eventually, by yawning widely and feigning sleep, she had managed to stop Gaynor talking. But long after Gaynor's breathing had settled into a gentle, even rhythm, Beth was still staring at the ceiling. When at last she slid into fitful sleep, she dreamed of Allan, disjointed dreams, full of anger and accusation.

She had woken once, in the early hours, filled with a terrible, aching sadness, but had drifted off again and was deeply asleep when Hofi knocked on the door, telling them breakfast would be ready in ten minutes.

'We'll be stopping at Godafoss,' Allan announced, turning his head so that they could all hear. 'Waterfalls are one of Iceland's most beautiful features, and in the summer they are at their most spectacular.'

'Great,' Gaynor nodded enthusiastically and sat back.

Taking her camera out of its leather case she turned to Beth, mouthing, 'Why?'

Beth wondered why she hadn't asked Allan, then realised that for all her apparent sophistication, Gaynor was awed by Allan, and didn't want to appear ignorant. 'In the winter many of them ice up and the flow is severely restricted,' she explained softly, checking the settings on her camera. 'But in summer they are carrying all the extra water from the melting snow as well as from the glaciers.'

Gaynor gave her a grateful nod.

Allan pulled in behind Gunnar and everyone climbed out. Bare patches of rock and brown earth showing through the sparse grass were evidence of the slow growth of vegetation at this northerly latitude.

Eugene hurried over. 'You getting pictures, Beth?'

'I'm just about to,' she replied. 'Would you like to stand over there by that large boulder? You'll be in the centre of the shot with the falls behind you.'

Eugene beamed and shouted for Lucille to join him.

The wide mouth of the falls was divided by two thick pillars of grass-topped rock resembling teeth, which stood almost in the centre of the roaring cascade. Eugene's bright red sweater and Lucille's of grey and yellow stood out against the backdrop of white foam and sapphire water.

Beth took two shots, signalling her approval to Eugene with a circle of thumb and forefinger. She turned back to the Land Rover in time to see Allan's dark head bent close to Gaynor's blonde one as he did something to her camera then handed it back. Flashing him a dazzling smile, Gaynor asked him a question. He shook his head, making a negative gesture with one hand.

Quickly hiding her evident disappointment, Gaynor beckoned to Rob, who rushed forward like an eager puppy, and together they walked over the uneven ground towards the cliff-edge, arguing cheerfully about who should actually take the picture.

As they passed Beth, she couldn't help asking, 'Problems with the camera?'

'The lens cap sitcks,' Gaynor grimaced, 'and I'm terrified if I force it I'll break something.' Then, out of Rob's view, she gave Beth a huge conspiratorial wink.

Beth bit the inside of her lip and started towards Hofi who was leaning back against the bonnet, her arms folded, her face turned up to the sun, and asked, 'Are we having coffee here?'

Allan stood a few feet away, talking to Gunnar. At the sound of her voice he looked over his shoulder. 'This isn't a luxury cruise. We've only been on the road just over an hour.'

The censure in his tone touched her on the raw, but Beth managed to keep her voice even. 'I wasn't suggesting we *should*, it was simply a request for information.'

'Well then, for your information,' he mocked, 'we are not stopping for coffee or tea-breaks. We will have lunch at Myvatn and make camp for the night on the far side of Namaskard. We'll be there between three and four,' he said. Then, correctly interpreting her look of surprise but giving her no chance to interrupt, he went on, 'Erecting the tents and establishing a routine always takes longer on the first day. In any case, as Namaskard is a high-temperature activity area, Eugene will expect you to start earning your place on this expedition.'

'Thank you,' Beth said with acid sweetness, 'that was all I wanted to know.'

Gunnar's face was clouded with concern and uncertainty and he looked helplessly at his wife, but Hofi, with an imperceptible shake of her head smiled at Beth. 'Did you see Strokkur when you were in the south?'

Beth nodded, grateful for Hofi's tactful change of subject. 'It was fantastic. I got some marvellous shots of it in action. The column of water must have shot a hundred feet into the air. Hofi, why doesn't Geysir spout any more?'

Hofi shrugged sadly. 'The geologists are not sure. It could be that with new springs erupting in the area, the pressure has changed. But it is possible the tourists choked it to death.'

Beth looked startled. 'How?'

'A geyser is unpredictable. But it is possible to provoke it into erupting by breaking the surface tension of the water when it is still. You toss in a small stone and *whoosh*. Perhaps too many people, too impatient to wait for it to blow naturally, tried to force it.' She spread her hands. 'Now Geysir, after giving his name to hot springs all over the world, is only a flat pool.'

They were quiet for a moment, then Hofi prompted, 'What else did you see?'

Beth sighed and made a wry face. 'It would be easier to tell you what I *didn't* see. When I wasn't eating, sleeping or taking photographs, I was on the move. I went to the village where coffee bushes and banana palms are grown in greenhouses heated by hot springs. I saw outwash plains, great expanses of gravel washed down from the glaciers, glacial lagoons like giant mirrors with icebergs floating on them. The rock bridges and formations at Dyrholaey were fascinating.'

'What about the bird colonies?' Hofi asked. 'And did you see any seals?'

Beth nodded. 'And gannets, and puffins. And I was attacked by skuas. That was unnerving. I was at least twenty yards from the nests. It was like something out of that Hitchcock film "The Birds."'

'What did you enjoy most?'

Following Hofi's example, Beth was leaning back against the side of the Land Rover. Her head tilted back, eyes closed, she soaked up the sun's warmth, unaware that Gunnar had gone to call Rob, Gaynor, Eugene and Lucille back to the vehicles, and that Allan stood only a few feet away, resting his foot on a rock as he retied his bootlaces.

'It was all marvellous,' Beth replied. 'I love this country. But

most? I think . . . the day I spent at a beach on the south coast.'
Her voice softened. 'I don't even remember what it was
called.'

'What made it special?' Hofi asked. 'Did you have
company?'

'No,' Beth said quietly. 'I was completely alone. It had
rained heavily the night before and lots of tours had changed
their itineraries because of difficulties at the river crossings.
But I had stayed the night in a small village. It was still very
windy and the sea was rough. There were some incredible
cloud formations, and the contrast between the black volcanic
sand, white surf, and turquoise water was absolutely
beautiful.'

Allan had finished tying his boot, and stood head bent,
immobile, not wanting to listen, unable to walk away as Hofi
asked, 'What do you think about when you're on your own?'
She sounded lazily curious. 'Do you just let your mind
wander?'

Beth gave a deep sigh. It caught in her throat like a tiny sob.
Allan's lips compressed in a thin bitter line and his fingers
curved into his palms. Beneath Beth's closed eyelids
unexpected tears welled up.

'Oh, no,' she murmured, 'I can't afford to . . . ' But she had
that day, just for a while, until the pain had become
unbearable and, alone on the wide beach, with the waves
thundering, she had wept. A single scalding tear slid from
between her lids and down over her cheekbone.

'You mean——?' Hofi sounded hopeful.

'No.' Beth didn't let her finish. 'I mean I always have too
much to think about. I'm just a single girl with a living to earn
and a professional reputation to build.' She swallowed
surreptitiously, hoping Hofi hadn't noticed the thickness in
her voice.

'I just thought——'

'Don't, Hofi,' Beth's voice, still quiet, grew sharper. 'I—it's pointless.'

She straightened up, opening her eyes. Allan stood less than a yard away, his features a bleak mask.

Turning away as Beth stifled a gasp, he strode to the second vehicle and banged on the metal side. 'Let's go!'

During the next hour and a half, as the road climbed through mountains with even higher, snow-capped, peaks behind them, Beth was careful to avoid the rear-view mirror. She knew Allan looked at her from time to time. She could sense when his eyes were on her. But why? He had made it perfectly plain she was the last person in the world he had any desire to see. She felt exactly the same about him.

So why was it that even the briefest exchange of glances could penetrate her carefully built defences and sweep them aside like so much dust?

Was he aware of the effect he was having on her? If he was, and she kept denying it to both him and herself, he would continue to bait and harass her. There was no doubt he intended to make her pay for being there.

In her shock, she had been simply *reacting*, instead of thinking things out. It might be necessary to pretend to the others that she and Allan were strangers, but it was foolish to try and pretend to herself.

She had to face facts. She had lived with Allan, loved and been loved by him. They had been as close, physically and emotionally, as it was possible for a man and a woman to be. *Or so she had believed.* Yet the fact that there had been a part of his life she knew nothing about did not alter what they *had* shared.

Instead of wasting vital energy denying the past, she had to face it openly and accept it. Only then would he have no further hold over her.

'You're quiet, Beth,' Rob broke into her thoughts, making her start. 'Not travel-sick, are you?' He sounded sympathetic.

Immediately, Gaynor opened her bag and poked about

among the contents.

'Of course she's not,' Allan said impatiently.

Rob and Gaynor both looked at him in surprise. Beth's heart skipped a beat.

'Miss Farrell is a seasoned traveller,' Allan said smoothly. 'It's part of her job.'

This time Beth couldn't resist a swift glance in the mirror. But Allan kept his eyes on the road and Beth felt a sharp stab of satisfaction. The slip had been accidental. It was only a tiny crack in his formidable armour, but she had seen it, and it gave her new strength.

'Well, just in case anyone does feel queasy, I brought some Dramamine,' Gaynor said, still rummaging. 'And a cologne stick. My grandma used to swear by those.' She produced the blue plastic cylinder with a flourish. 'I've carried this ever since I had my first grown-up bag. I've never used it. Seems to me, the more you're prepared, the less likely you are to need any of this stuff.' She gave a laughing grimace and Beth couldn't help smiling with her.

'Anyhow, what's with all this 'Miss Farrell' stuff? Don't you two like each other?' Gaynor's lovely eyes were speculative. For a moment Beth had forgotten how shrewd she could be.

Beth and Allan exchanged a brief glance, but before Beth could say a word Allan was already speaking.

'How can you dislike someone you don't know? The formality was sheer force of habit on my part. From now on it's Beth and Allan, just like old friends. Right, Beth?'

His eyes, as they met hers in the mirror, glittered strangely and Beth felt a renewed sense of threat. But with Rob and Gaynor watching her, she had no choice but to stretch her mouth into a smile. 'Of course . . . Allan.'

For the sake of something to do, Beth rubbed a little of the cologne on the insides of her wrists. It was refreshing. As she handed the stick back, Gaynor murmured in a tone that was half-joke, half-plea, 'Not *too* friendly.'

A while later they approached Myvatn.

'Gee, look at all those birds,' Gaynor pointed excitedly. 'I've never seen so many.'

'Myvatn means Midge Lake,' Allan explained. 'You'll see why when we get out,' he added drily. 'But they don't bite and it's because of them that this is the favourite breeding ground for hundreds of different species of water bird.'

Gaynor was leaning on the front seats again, her face alive with interest, though Beth would not have wanted to bet on whether the interest was in what Allan was telling them, or in Allan himself.

'Those craters look very small.' Rob indicated three grassy depressions between the road and the lake. 'Are they volcanic?'

Allan nodded. 'Yes, but they are not magna-fed. They were caused by hot lava flowing over wet ground. The water was turned to steam by the intense heat, and exploded through the bubble of lava. The crater was formed when the thin lava crust collapsed in on itself.'

Almost against her will, Beth found herself drawn forward, wanting to hear, to learn. During their time together, she had listened to Allan for hours, begging him to go on talking long after he would have stopped, fascinated by the scope of his knowledge.

Once, just before their wedding, she had been sitting on the rug at his feet as they relaxed by the fire, alone for once in the chalet they shared with the rest of the team. Her head on his knee, his fingers playing through her hair, he had broken off in mid-sentence and leaned forward, laughingly accusing her of only wanting him for his mind.

Her swift denial had been uttered before she realised, and blushed crimson. He had planted a lingering kiss on her mouth and for the next hour they had not talked much at all.

'There are some interesting lava formations on the far side of the lake,' Allan was saying to Rob. 'We'll take a look at them after lunch. Eugene will want to see them and I expect he'll want pictures.'

Beth's tentative plan for avoiding Allan during the stop by concentrating on the birds and plant-life crumbled.

'Can I come too?' Gaynor asked eagerly.

Allan threw her a quizzical glance. 'I didn't realise you were interested in geology.' Beth winced inwardly at his undertone of scepticism.

Gaynor went a deeper shade of pink but shrugged disarmingly. 'I don't want to miss anything.'

'Then come by all means.' Allan drew in behind Gunnar.

Desperate for a few moments alone, Beth took her lunch with her and went to get some close-ups of a few of the rarer birds and some plants she did not recognise. But, all too soon, Eugene was shouting to her, and, leaving Hofi washing up and Gunnar under the bonnet looking for the cause of a minor rattle, Beth passed Lucille perched on a rock near the water's edge, sketching a pair of whooper swans and their cygnets, and followed Allan, Gaynor, and Rob to the south side of the lake.

An hour later they were back on the road. Rob and Gaynor chattered brightly, he trying to impress her, she trying to impress Allan; neither noticing that Beth and Allan had withdrawn into a thoughtful silence.

'Hey, what's all that smoke?' Gaynor pointed to the huge clouds of vapour billowing into the air from a large building.

'It's not smoke, it's steam,' Allan replied with unexpected terseness.

'It's a diatomite factory,' Rob explained.

Gaynor looked blank. 'What are they?'

'The skeletal remains of minute plants. See those buoys? They mark where a pipe carries the diatoms from the lake bed to settling ponds behind the factory. They are used as filtering material by the chemical industries in Europe.'

'Is that so?' Gaynor sounded impressed.

Beth leaned forward. 'Allan, may we stop a moment?' She hadn't even noticed the factory, being far more intrigued by the wisps and streams of vapour coming up from cracks in the pale-coloured ground near the road.

Without answering, Allan unhooked the microphone and spoke into it briefly, then pulled the Land Rover to a stop on the right-hand side of the road.

'What's wrong?' Gaynor said.

'Nothing.' Beth reassured her. 'I just want to get some photographs. This is a geothermal area.'

Leaving Rob to explain what that was, she seized her camera and jumped out. Allan followed, slamming the door behind him.

'Be careful.' He was brusque. 'According to Gunnar some new fissures have opened up. That light-coloured clay isn't safe to walk on.'

She glanced round at him, her face unguarded, revealing her surprise at his apparent concern.

His features hardened. 'If the clay gives way, you get scalded by super-heated steam. Arranging your transfer to hospital would cause the expedition unnecesary delay.'

Beth flinched as though he had struck her. Her fingers tightened on the camera. 'Then I'll certainly take great care,' she retorted. 'It wouldn't do to cause you any inconvenience.'

His glare was icy. 'How considerate. But haven't you left it a little late?' His voice was perfectly controlled, but she sensed in him a pent-up violence that shook her.

Without giving her a chance to reply he turned away. 'Take your photographs,' he gritted and strolled back to the Land Rover.

It was mid-afternoon when they reached Namaskard. Below the eastern flank of a mountain whose rocky slopes were coloured brown, red, orange, yellow and white by the geothermal activity beneath, lay an area of sulphur pits, pools of bubbling blue-grey mud, and jets of super-heated steam which erupted from vents in the pale ground.

'Wow!' Gaynor wrinkled her nose at the powerful smell.

Rob, as always, was by her side. 'Not exactly the perfumes of Araby,' he grinned.

Gaynor's face contorted in distaste. 'It's just like rotten eggs.'

'Hydrogen sulphide gas, actually. Mind those holes,' he warned quickly, seizing her arm and drawing her away as she ventured too close to the hissing steam, 'that vapour contains hydrochloric acid, among other things.'

Gaynor gave a little wail and clung to his arm. Rob found it hard to conceal his delight.

With strangely mixed feelings, Beth turned away. Eugene was approaching her, making wide, arm-spreading gestures. Beth gave him a thumbs-up and changed direction. She knew without being told that he wanted as many different shots as possible of this alien landscape. She wanted to work alone, without him watching over her or offering well-meant but superfluous advice.

She crouched down beside one of the largest mud pools. It was three yards across, with a yard-high rim, formed by the splattering mud. The liquid mud slurped noisily as the large bubbles of gas popped.

Beth got two marvellous shots, one with a foot-wide bubble rising into a dome, the second just as it burst and a circle of droplets hung in mid-air.

She walked on towards a cream-coloured cone from which steam was billowing like a mini-volcano. The stench was sickly-sweet, and the mouth of the cone was stained yellow by the powdered sulphur. She took two more shots from different angles.

From the corner of her eye, Beth noticed Allan leave the group and start towards her. *What now?* She pretended she hadn't seen him and, re-setting her camera, moved across to an oddly shaped fissure. Why didn't he leave her alone? She wasn't bothering him. She just wanted to be left in peace to do her job.

Blue, green, orange and red crystals spilled from the mouth of the fissure, glistening like jewel-encrusted cushions in the sunshine. Beth was entranced. She crouched, sitting on one heel, her other knee bent, focusing on the dazzling shapes and colours, adjusting the lens so that each crystal was sharp-edged and clear, and took several shots.

She was vaguely aware of a thudding sound behind her, but ignored it. All her concentration was directed through the view-finder.

The crystals grew cloudy, as though someone had breathed on them, and a sudden waft of gas caught in her throat, making her cough. She lowered the camera to wipe her eyes and the lens. Without warning she was hurled sideways, and sprawled full-length on the hard ground, grunting as all the breath was knocked out of her.

Automatically raising the hand that held her camera to prevent it being smashed, her forearm jarred sickeningly against a rock.

Unable to move for the warm, heavy weight pinning her down, Beth dazed and shocked, twisted her head round, and gasped.

Grabbing her head, Allan forced it into the hollow between his neck and shoulder and brought his own down close.

As she began to struggle, his grip tightened. 'Shut up,' he snarled. 'Keep still.'

Warned by something in his voice, Beth obeyed. And then she heard it, a faint roaring, growing louder and louder. She could feel the ground vibrating beneath her and flaring anxiety knotted her stomach and dried her mouth.

With a noise like an express train, super-heated gas and steam exploded from the fissure. Had Beth still been crouched over the opening, the blast would have caught her full in the face.

With a strangled whimper she hunched against Allan. The eruption seemed endless. Condensing droplets rained down around them, stinging as they landed on the bare flesh of Beth's outstretched arm. Then it stopped, the noise faded, and there was silence. But neither moved.

Overwhelmed by the horror of what might have been, Beth was struggling to come to terms with the fact that it was *Allan* who had saved her, whose body was protecting hers, *the same Allan who had so cynically betrayed her.* Her head ached with confusion.

Tensely, she waited for his fury to break, knowing she deserved whatever curses he hurled at her. Still he did not speak.

His body was hard and unyielding, as if every nerve, every muscle, had been drawn tight. His breathing was harsh and warm against her face and neck. Beth felt his fingers tighten in her hair. Then from a long way off came thudding footsteps and shouts as the others ran towards them.

With a barely audible sound, a catching of breath deep in his throat, Allan rolled away from her and stiffly, Beth sat up.

Wiping dust and grit from her face and right shoulder, she cleared a sudden hoarseness from her throat, and the question that had been hammering away at her subconscious finally broke through. 'Why didn't you shout?' she asked softly.

He glanced up, his eyes smoke-dark. 'You wouldn't have moved in time.' His voice was cool, matter-of-fact.

Not couldn't, *wouldn't.* He was right, and they both knew it. She would have ignored him, pretended not to hear. And she might have been badly, if not fatally, injured.

Gunnar and Rob arrived, with Eugene, Hofi and Gaynor right behind and Lucille puffing up in the rear.

After reassuring them all that she was perfectly all right, Beth eased herself free of the helping hands and turned towards Allan who stood slightly apart, absently brushing the dust from his trousers.

'I—I owe you an apology.' Her voice had a slight tremor.

His eyes blazed fiercely. 'You owe me a hell of a lot more

than that,' he hissed, his lips barely moving, and icy fingers clamped around her heart.

'My God, Beth,' Gaynor shrieked, 'your arm!'

Beth looked down, bending her elbow, and was mildly surprised by the huge red and purple bruise that stretched almost the length of her swollen forearm. Blood from several cuts and grazes had dried in dark runnels.

Hofi put her arm around Beth's shoulders. 'Come, I get the first-aid kit.'

'It looks worse than it is,' Beth said, 'honestly.' She was near to tears and couldn't understand why.

'How about your camera?' Eugene was still trying to regain his breath, his forehead furrowed in anxiety. 'Is it OK? Did you damage the film?'

Hofi snorted softly in indignation and Beth bit her lip. She felt light-headed, her control precarious. If she started laughing she might not be able to stop.

She held out the camera she had been clutching to her chest. 'It's fine, Eugene. No damage.'

Lucille nudged him hard and Beth heard him muttering in justification, 'Well, she's got some great stuff on there. She can't go back and do it again.'

Can't go back . . . can't go back. The words echoed inside Beth's head. She glanced over her shoulder. Her eyes met Allan's for an instant, then Hofi drew her away towards the Land Rover and the first-aid kit.

CHAPTER FIVE

HANGING low in the western sky, the sun cast long shadows over the undulating ground with its close-cropped carpet of grass. The hills were bathed in mellow light, and small glaciers on the mountains beyond spilled from the summits like gleaming gold ribbons. A few yards away a stream chuckled swiftly over its rocky bed, the sparkling water ice-cold.

Tents and suitcases had been unloaded and, inside the mobile kitchen, Hofi was already busy.

Crouched beside the unfolded tent, slotting the supporting poles together, Beth's mouth watered as the smell of frying onions wafted across their camp site.

At Hofi's request Gaynor was lending a hand with the meal. Beth had been relieved to see her go. Several times she had caught Gaynor watching her and she sensed that behind the speculative gaze more and more questions were forming.

'How're you doing?' Rob's cheerful enquiry brought her head up.

'Fine thanks.' She smiled at him.

'I thought you might be able to use an extra hand getting the tent up. How is it feeling now?' He gestured towards her arm.

Beth glanced at the bandage stretching from wrist to elbow. 'A bit sore,' she admitted, adding quickly, 'and don't tell me how lucky I was.' She gave a wry grimace. 'I know better than anyone what a stupid, dangerous risk I took. My only excuse is that I honestly didn't realise it at the time. Which wouldn't have counted for much if I'd had my head blown off.'

Despite the attempted joke, Beth's skin crawled and she could not suppress a shudder as, once more, the realisation washed over her of just how close to death she had been.

Rob raised both hands in mock surrender. 'OK, OK, I can see you've learned your lesson.'

'And how!' Beth's agreement was heartfelt.

'Mind you,' he confided, 'that was a terrific flying tackle by our esteemed leader. He should have played rugby for England.'

'He did,' Beth said without thinking. Then as Rob's eyebrows disappeared beneath his untidy fringe, she stammered, 'Er—Hofi mentioned it. She and Gunnar had known him quite a while. He used to play at university apparently.'

'Aaahh,' Rob nodded thoughtfully, his gaze fixed on Beth's flushed cheeks.

She dived into the tent to fix the poles in place. 'If you're here to help, peg the guy-ropes in,' she called, and in a desperate effort to change the subject, blurted, 'What did you think of Dettifoss?'

'For the most powerful waterfall in Europe, with a drop of a hundred and forty feet, carrying one hundred and ninety tons of water a second,' he shouted back, 'I'd say it isn't half bad.'

Inside the tent, Beth grinned. Rob was a tonic. She crawled out, and they continued the banter, laughing and teasing one another, as they hammered tent pegs into the stony ground and tightened the ropes.

'Oh-oh,' Rob muttered, looking over Beth's shoulder then shooting her a cryptic glance. 'Allan Bryce is on his way over and methinks his mood doth leave room for improvement.'

Beth felt all her nerves contract. She caught herself and straightened up, lifting her chin, forcing herself to relax.

Speaking directly to Rob, Allan said, 'I wonder if you'd mind giving Gunnar a hand.' His tone was pleasant but his expression made it clear he was issuing an order rather than making a request.

Tossing aside the stone he had been using as a hammer, Rob dusted his hands off. 'Sure,' he said. 'What needs doing?'

A cool smile lifted the corners of Allan's mouth. 'I expect he'll tell you as soon as you get there.'

As Rob turned to go, he caught Beth's eye and the wealth of meaning in his look deepened the pinkness in her cheeks.

Allan waited, watching until Rob was several yards, away, then swung back to Beth. His features had hardened and his eyes glittered beneath narrowed lids. 'You seem to be getting on well with young Wilson,' he observed tersely.

His reference to Rob as 'young Wilson', when there couldn't be more than three years difference in their ages, brought a smile to Beth's lips. 'I am,' she agreed. 'He's a lot of fun.'

Her smile appeared to provoke Allan, who announced frostily, 'He's here to work.'

'I thought we all were.' Beth's chin rose a fraction. 'I have no desire or intention of interfering with his work. But surely a little light relief when we're——'

'Just don't lead the poor bastard on,' he snapped. His eyes ablaze with seething emotions he could no longer conceal, he turned on his heel.

'*What?*' Beth felt her colour drain away, she couldn't have heard him correctly. Then it flooded back as scalding rage filled her. He dared say that to her after what *he* had done?

'Just what the hell are you getting at?'

Allan glanced back, once more in perfect control, his expression icily disdainful. 'Surely it's plain enough?'

'It's *ridiculous*.' Beth glared at him. 'I only met Rob yesterday, for heaven's sake. And for your information, I have never in my life led anyone on. Rob and I are not the least bit interested in each other romantically, if that is what you are insinuating. Not that it would be any of *your* business if we were.'

Allan's face darkened. 'None of my business?' he rasped. 'We were married, you and I. Or have you conveniently forgotten about that?'

It was a brutal shock, hearing him actually say it. He had treated her as a stranger, with far less friendliness than he had shown any of the others. Why had he thrown that at her? What did it have to do with now?'

'Forgotten?' Beth whispered. 'God knows I've tried.' She lifted her chin defiantly. 'It might have been your idea of marriage,' she flung at him, 'it certainly wasn't mine. Honesty and trust are important to me. To you they are irrelevant.' She drew herself up. 'And as far as Rob is concerned, he has fallen rather hard for Gaynor. Which makes two of you.'

The instant she uttered those last words she knew they were a mistake. She would never have gone so far, or let him know that she had noticed, if he had not goaded her beyond endurance.

Allan was clearly startled, but Beth was too busy trying to regain her own self-possession to wonder what she had said that had shaken him.

He recovered swiftly and one dark brow lifted in derision. 'Jealous?' he queried softly.

Beth remembered all the anguish she had suffered, her grief as the realisation dawned that those precious intimacies they had shared, stored in her memory like priceless treasures, were worthless. That even while telling her he loved her, that she was the most important thing ever to happen in his life, he had merely been using her with a cruel cynicism that defied belief. She remembered the bitterness which, for a while, had threatened to overwhelm her.

'No,' she said flatly, 'I'm not jealous. I'd say Gaynor is welcome to you, except that Rob would be far better for her, and I'd be sorry to see her hurt. Excuse me.' She turned and bent to pick up her case and take it into the tent. But Allan seized her arm, hauling her upright, his face a mask of fury.

'You think *you* have a monopoly on pain?' he grated. 'Don't you have any idea of what *I* went through?' His face was pale, his features drawn. The fingers biting into the flesh of her upper arm trembled with the force of his anger.

'No, I don't.' Beth's voice was hoarse with stress. 'Perhaps if I'd another husband I'd kept secret from you, I might——'

'This isn't finished,' he gritted, releasing her suddenly and thrusting both hands into his pockets.

Beth stumbled back a pace. 'You're wrong.' She glared at him. 'If finished two years ago.'

But Allan had already turned away and was walking back towards his own tent.

At a loss, Beth gently rubbed her throbbing arm. Why had he left so abruptly? Then, reaching for her suitcase, she saw Gaynor standing by the open door of the mobile kitchen from which she had evidently just emerged. Uncertainty clouded her lovely features as Allan strode past without a word or glance.

Beth had taken out her pyjamas, toilet bag and towel, and was unrolling her sleeping-bag when Gaynor poked her head into the tent.

'Hofi wants you.'

Beth glanced round. 'Right, thanks.'

Gaynor crawled in, dragging her case behind her. 'What do we do for a bathroom?'

'Hofi and Gunnar usually bring a chemical loo, it's got

its own tent. I expect Gunnar has set it up somewhere behind the Land Rover. As for a wash, we'll have to make do with a bucket or the washing-up bowl. There's always the stream, but that's awfully cold. I'll ask Hofi if she'll boil us some water after supper.'

'Sure.' Gaynor was subdued.

Beth hesitated, wondering whether to ask if anything was wrong. But, guessing that would only open the floodgates to Gaynor's questions, she bit her tongue and crawled out.

'Everything under control?' she asked Hofi, stepping up into the tiny caravan-like trailer lined with cupboards. Pans bubbled on the gas burners and a large plate of cold meat lay on the folding flap that served as a work-surface. There was just enough room for them both.

'Gaynor is asking many questions.' Hofi unlatched one of the cupboards and took down plates and bowls.

'About me?' Beth bit her lip.

Hofi nodded. 'And about Allan.'

'What have you told her?'

'Very little.' Hofi lifted one of the saucepan lids and stirred the contents. 'I speak of your work, of his work. That is not what she wants. She is shy to ask more now, but soon she will. Soon I will have to tell her you still love each other.'

'Hofi, that's crazy and you know it,' Beth snapped crossly.

Hofi turned and caught Beth's hands. 'Is it?' she demanded gently. 'Allan saved your life today.'

'I know that and I'm grateful,' Beth said. 'But me being splattered all over the area wouldn't exactly have enhanced his reputation as an expedition leader.'

'You think he did it for himself?' Hofi tutted and shook her head. 'You did not see the look on his face when he realised what was about to happen. He himself could have been badly injured. He would have lost the consultancy post. He wants that job very much. But none of that was in his mind. He thought only of you.'

'I suppose he told you that?' Beth asked and when Hofi's lashes fluttered down she sighed. 'I know you mean well, Hofi, but it's no good. You are seeing what you want to see, not the truth.'

Perhaps,' Hofi murmured, 'but if I am so foolish, maybe you will tell me why Allan try to stop you being friends with Rob?'

Beth blinked, then shrugged helplessly. 'He's angry that I'm here. It's his way of getting at me.'

'Aaah,' Hofi nodded. 'So it cannot be that he is jealous.'

'Allan? Jealous?' Beth's laugh held no humour. 'I am nothing to him but an irritation, a reminder of a past we would both prefer to forget.'

'So because he hate you and want you out of his mind, he risk *his* life to save yours.' Hofi shook her head. 'It make not much sense to me.'

'Your English is falling apart,' Beth half grinned, attempting to lighten the atmosphere, but Hofi would not be distracted. She slammed the cutlery drawer shut after extracting knives, forks and spoons.

'Is not a joke, Beth. You tell me you leave Allan because he already have a wife. Is not true.'

'You think I'd lie to you?' Beth stared at her friend.

'No, no,' Hofi said impatiently. 'But is not true he have a *wife*. I ask Gunnar. Gunnar and Allan are good friends, they know each other many years. Gunnar say Allan is not married. He have no wife until he marry you.'

'Hofi, I don't care what Gunnar says, I *saw* her,' Beth retorted wretchedly. 'She came to Allan's flat. We had only been back from our honeymoon . . . ' She broke off, biting the inside of her lip. 'Anyway, I answered the door and she asked who I was. When I told her I was Allan's wife she laughed. She was beautiful, but strange, almost hysterical, as though she was under some dreadful strain.' Beth's voice faltered. 'I guess she must have been. Then she said *I* couldn't be his wife because *she* was. She gave me a letter for him and disappeared.'

Hofi stared at her, stunned, then wrapped an arm around Beth's shoulders and hugged her, murmuring in Icelandic. 'My poor Beth,' she reverted to English. 'What did you say to him?'

'Nothing,' Beth whispered. 'I had packed my case and gone before he got back.' She looked up at her friend. 'What else could I have done, Hofi?' she beseeched. 'What sort of man would *do* a thing like that?' Disbelief choked her now as it had then. 'We went through a wedding ceremony. He declared in front of witnesses that there was no barrier to our marriage.' She shook her head incredulously. 'And all the time he had a wife.'

'So you did not see him again? To talk?'

'What was there to say?' Beth swallowed painfully. 'He had lied to me, Hofi. What would have been the point of listening to more lies? I spent most of my childhood watching my mother do that. She tried to pretend everything was all right when it quite obviously wasn't. Believing my father when he said it wouldn't happen again, only it always did.'

'Oh, Beth, I am so sorry.' Hofi held her friend close. 'I did not know.'

Beth gave her a watery smile. 'How could you? I've never told a living soul. You see, they'd been married twelve years before I was born. I was their only child. They both loved me very much and I wanted for nothing. But my arrival meant that my mother no longer accompanied my father on business trips abroad as she always had done in the past. Dad had a good job and as Mum neither needed or wanted to go out to work, I became the centre of her life.'

Beth's mouth softened. 'Each time he came back from a trip Dad would bring armfuls of toys and pretty clothes for me and masses of expensive presents for Mum.' Her face

grew strained. 'But as I grew older I began to associate his
return and the toys and gifts with raised voices behind
closed doors and accusations I didn't understand. Mum's
eyes would be swollen and red, and Dad would go into
long, brooding silences. My school work suffered. I
couldn't concentrate. I loved them both, yet divided loyalty
and feelings of guilt were tearing me apart. It seemed to be
somehow *my* fault that they weren't happy.

'When I was eleven they sent me to boarding-school. I
missed them both dreadfully to begin with, but in a way it
was a relief to be away from the rows. If I wasn't there, I
wasn't responsible.'

'Were you happy at the new school?' Hofi asked.

'It took a while to settle in,' Beth admitted. 'It was an
entirely different way of life.' She had cried herself to sleep
for a week, but had soon learned to hide her vulnerability
behind a proctective mask of aloofness and self-possession.

'What about the holidays? Did you go home?'

Beth nodded. 'I was worried sick the first time,
wondering what I'd find and how they would be. As it
happened it was the best holiday we'd ever spent. They had
just come back from a trip to the States and seemed happier
than I could ever remember. But my mother never quite
lost the lines of strain and misery around her eyes. And
though I loved my father dearly and came to understand the
reason for his *affaires*, deep inside me all the unhappiness I
had witnessed as a child crystallised into a determination
never to permit such a thing to happen to me.'

Beth looked down at her clenched fists. 'Allan did not
simply have an *affaire*. He was *married* to someone else.
Nothing he said could possibly have excused that.'

'Beth,' Hofi began tentatively, 'I do not excuse him, he
has caused you much pain but . . . might there have been a
reason? Something which, while not condoning his actions,
might at least have explained?'

Beth's head jerked up. She had not waited to find out. The paralysing shock had resurrected all the vivid memories of her childhood and, *like a child, she had run away*. She had never viewed it like that before. She didn't want to now, for it put her in the wrong and she wasn't. *Was she?* 'A—At least I didn't have to go through a divorce. I couldn't have faced having the whole miserable mess aired in a public court.' At Hofi's perplexed expression she explained. 'A bigamous marriage is null and void. In the law it never existed, so there is nothing to dissolve.'

'Then the first time you are speaking to each other——'

'Was when he walked into your kitchen yesterday evening,' Beth finished, and drew in a long shaky breath.

Hofi nodded slowly, clearly finding it difficult to absorb all she had just heard. 'I think we eat now. It has been, as you say, quite a day.'

Beth's mouth twisted in weary agreement. 'You can say that again.'

After the meal, which they ate sitting on the ground in a circle, Lucille made the coffee while Gaynor started clearing up the dishes. Hofi disappeared into the loo tent and when she emerged a while later she looked a little pale. Beth noticed but thought no more of it and, fetching her camera, took shots of the camp-site and everyone busy at their allotted tasks. Then she swapped the wide-angle lens for a macro and, moving a little further away, stretched out on the ground to take some close-ups of rock textures and a tiny yellow flower growing in a crevice between two boulders.

Allan and Gunnar were running the daily check on the vehicles, tightening wheel nuts loosened by vibration due to the rough roads and tracks. They examined the exhaust pipes and hangers, and tested levels of coolant and engine oil.

Rob and Eugene had been given the task of putting transparent sticky tape over the head and tail-lights to reduce the risk of their being shattered by loose stones.

When Beth eventually returned to the tent, the entrance was blocked by a bucket of soapy water. Inside, her hair loose and freshly brushed, Gaynor was pulling on her mink-lined jacket over a cream silk pyjama top.

'It's all yours.' She indicated the cramped, untidy space. 'Momma wants to talk to me. I expect it's about Dr Bryce.' As Beth's head came up, Gaynor went on lightly, 'My mom is a great matchmaker, and she's got this idea Allan would make a good husband for me.'

Somehow Beth kept her voice devoid of all expression as she automatically folded and stacked the clothes Gaynor had strewn across both sleeping-bags. 'How do you feel about that?'

Gaynor shrugged, her half-smile forlorn. 'I don't know.' Her face brightened for a moment. 'I think he's gorgeous. I mean, who wouldn't?' She looked thoughtful. 'But he doesn't give the impression of being available. Anyway, my track-record isn't too good. I've already had two husbands.'

Beth nodded sympathetically. 'Your mother did mention it.'

Gaynor's laugh was bitter and hurt. 'She never loses an opportunity to *mention* it. And what about my daddy? Did he just *mention* all the money he'd spent on my education, and the braces for my teeth, and the corrective eye surgery so I wouldn't have to wear glasses, because that would have lessened my chances in the marriage market?'

Beth was taken aback. 'N—No. Surely he wouldn't——'

'You don't know my daddy,' Gaynor said in her soft, husky voice. 'Once a cattleman, always a cattleman. I was his prize heifer. He corrected all the visible flaws and sold me to the highest bidder.'

Beth was openly shocked, but Gaynor went on explaining, her tone quite matter-of-fact. 'He and Momma had brought me up to be obedient and respectful, and to believe that they knew what was best for me. Who was I to argue? What did I know? The men Daddy chose for me were young and wealthy and came from the top families in the state. The only trouble was they had flaws too, but no one warned me, and by the time I found out it was too late.'

She tugged the jacket around her as if she were suddenly cold. Beth had abandoned the tidying up and simply listened, understanding that Gaynor had been bottling all this up for a long, long time, and desperately needed to talk it out.

'My first husband, Jeff, was a computer salesman. He was one of the best, but competition between companies was cut-throat and Jeff had a problem handling the pressure. He snorted coke, and thought no party was a success unless you went home with someone else's wife . . . or husband.' Her voice fell. 'I couldn't take it, and he refused to let me get help for him.'

She examined her beautiful painted nails and heaved a sigh. 'Then there was Cal. He was in the oil business, a director of one of his daddy's companies. Cal didn't do drugs, he was into keeping fit. He jogged and played squash. He encouraged me to go to aerobics class. At one time I was going to four a week. What with that and the beauty parlour and the hairdresser I hardly had a moment to spare.' I should be so lucky, Beth thought wryly, but remained silent, for something told her Gaynor had not sought this apparent self-indulgence, it had been forced upon her.

'He always wanted me to look my best,' Gaynor went on. 'That was one of the reasons he didn't want us to have children. He liked his home and his wife to look perfect for the dinner guests he brought home two or three nights a week.' She fell silent, her head bent.

Beth searched desperately for something to say. 'That

must have been quite a challenge, planning all those different menus.'

Gaynor looked up, her eyes full of resignation. 'Cal didn't let me cook. He always had professional caterers supply everything,' her voice had an edge, 'even the flowers. Everyone said what a perfect couple we made, the young, successful oilman and his beautiful wife.'

She twisted a button on her jacket. 'We went to Hawaii for our honeymoon. Cal said it was the most romantic place on earth. I found out later he'd taken his secretary to the same hotel.'

Gaynor smiled sadly at Beth's sharp intake of breath. 'I could have coped with that. But when I found out that he was still sleeping with her . . . All our friends had known for months. It seems she and Cal had had something going for a couple of years. Then she had gone off with someone else and he had married me. But when her new relationship folded, she ran back to Cal, and he just couldn't say no.' Gaynor's eyes glistened with unshed tears. 'Everyone knew. Except me. I guess they all thought I *did* know and was just ignoring it. After all, I had a great life, no need to work, no responsibility, plenty of money and all the time in the world to spend prettying myself up for my husband and his friends.'

In a revealing, child-like gesture, Gaynor pressed her knuckles to her nose as she sniffed, then she tossed her head, flicking the hair back with a hopeless shrug. 'Maybe I should have stayed, then Daddy wouldn't be mad at me and Momma could stop worrying about the shame of her only daughter being unable to keep a husband.'

Beth shook her head. 'Couldn't you be misreading them? Surely they wouldn't have wanted you to stay with a man who was blatantly cheating on you? Maybe they're just concerned . . .' She broke off at Gaynor's pitying look.

'I was brought up to be a wife. As far as Daddy is concerned I've had two chances and blown them both.'

'But you couldn't have stayed married to either of those men,' Beth argued.

Gaynor shrugged again. 'Plenty do. But you're right, *I* couldn't. The problem is, what now! I sure as hell haven't been a wild success as a wife.' A wisecracking cynicism hardened her tone. 'Could be I'd make a better mistress.' She examined her nails again. 'There isn't a man born who can resist flattery. I bet if I really put my mind to it I could get Allan Bryce interested, despite the *keep-off* signals he's sending out.'

Beth was bemused. Keep-off signals? It hadn't looked like that to her. But then, she thought ironically, what would she know? Gaynor's experience of reading men was clearly far superior to hers.

Gaynor studied Beth, her wide blue eyes suddenly pensive, then she added softly, 'But I guess you wouldn't like that.'

Beth was fervently grateful for the dimness which hid the heat rising like a tidal wave up her throat to flood her face. She busied herself putting the folded clothes neatly into Gaynor's suitcase. 'What makes you think anything Allan Bryce does could possibly matter to me? I don't even like the man.'

'How can you dislike someone you don't know?' Gaynor quoted Allan's words back at her and Beth realised she had overdone it and betrayed herself.

'C'mon, Beth, there's something between you two. I'm not blind. And despite being a blonde, I'm no fool either.'

Beth saw total denial was pointless. 'We've met before, yes,' she admitted.

'I knew it.' Gaynor was quietly triumphant. 'I had a feeling about you two back at the Petursson place. And once we set off there was an awful lot of static between you. Were you close? I mean, did you know him well?'

Beth was quite still. Close? Oh yes, they had been close. Two halves of a whole, a perfect match. *Or so she had thought.* 'You know how it is,' she said lightly. 'You *think* you know someone. Then it turns out you didn't know them at all.'

'And now? I mean, meeting up again like this?'

Beth lifted one shoulder briefly. 'Neither of us had any idea the other would be here. It was pure coincidence, one of life's practical jokes.'

'So I wouldn't be trespassing?'

Beth forced herself to smile as she shook her head. Why was it so difficult?

Gaynor yawned and stretched sensuously, lifting the gleaming fall of hair off her neck. 'You know, Beth,' she confided, 'I could do with some *fun*. A flirtation maybe, or even an affair. I miss a man in my life.'

Once again Beth felt herself blush. Having few close girlfriends, she wasn't used to such frankness. Then the reality of what Gaynor meant hit her, and she bit back a gasp at the vicious pang caused by a fleeting, but all too vivid, image of Gaynor in Allan's arms, arms which had held *her*, which only this afternoon, despite their enmity, had enfolded her, protecting her as the steam vent erupted.

Quite unaware of Beth's inner struggle as she battled to convince herself it was only a knee-jerk reaction, that she really didn't care, Gaynor giggled. 'You know what? I quite fancy being a scarlet woman. Seems to me they have all the fun and none of the hassle.'

'I—I'd be a bit careful if I were you,' Beth managed, her throat dry. 'From what I know of Allan Bryce I wouldn't think he's a man to treat lightly. You might find you've got a tiger by the tail.'

'Wow,' Gaynor grinned. 'Sounds exciting.'

An expression of mild impatience flitted across Beth's face, lingering as an ironic twist on her gentle mouth. 'Oh yes, if that kind of excitement is what you want, all fizz and fireworks. The high would be terrific, while it *lasted*. Then, like a spent rocket, it would suddenly burn out and you'd crash back to earth. Is that really the sort of relationship you're looking for?'

Gaynor pouted. 'OK, Miss Wiseguy, do you have a better idea?'

'As a matter of fact, I do,' Beth said quietly. 'Rob may not have Allan Bryce's *charisma*, but he's fallen like a ton of bricks for you.'

Gaynor started, clearly surprised, and Beth realised that for all her assumed cynicism, the beautiful blonde was neither as confident nor as hard-boiled as she was trying to appear. 'He has? I thought it was all just talk.' She grimaced. 'And boy, does he talk.'

Beth bit back a smile. 'That's only because he's nervous,' she explained. 'He's trying to impress you.'

'He's wearing me out. Don't get me wrong,' she added quickly, 'it's not that I don't like him. I mean, what's there to *dislike*? He's not bad looking, he's a lot of laughs, but . . .' she spread her hands, 'there's something missing, you know?'

Beth knew all right. No other man would ever stir in her the exhilaration she had experienced with Allan's love-making. Gaynor was lucky, at least she didn't have that problem to surmount.

'That something might grow, if you give it a chance. There's a lot more to Rob than his sense of humour. He's kind, Gaynor, and he's a giver. There are precious few of those around these days. I don't suppose he's all that well off, though he must be good at his job or he wouldn't be on this project. The kind of giving I mean is thoughtfulness, consideration and caring. Rob would never deliberately hurt anyone.'

'You sound quite impressed with him yourself,' Gaynor

observed archly.

Beth grinned. 'I am, as a friend. I think he's terrific. But I'm not looking for romance right now.'

'Any special reason?'

Beth shook her head. 'I'm a career girl in a highly competitive business. I'm rarely in one place for long, and I have to work hard. I don't have much time or energy left over. Speaking of which, I really should try and get an early night. Didn't you say your mother was expecting you?'

'Oh, my God.' Gaynor clapped her hand to her mouth. 'I'd forgotten.' She pulled a face. 'She sure won't be too happy if I mess up her plans.'

'It's your life, Gaynor,' Beth pointed out, treading carefully. 'Instead of relying on other people's judgement, why not start trusting your own?'

'Well, I guess if this flops too, at least *I'll* have done the choosing, and not had him chosen for me.' She gave a crooked grin. 'Some consolation, huh?'

'Hey,' Beth chided, 'stop thinking failure. Rob thinks you're the best thing since sliced bread. All you have to do is relax, take one day at a time, get to know him a little better, then see how you feel. You don't have to rush into anything.'

'You're right,' Gaynor announced. 'That's just what I'm gonna do.' She contorted her face wryly, revealing a genuine unease about defying her mother, and crawled out of the tent.

Beth emptied the bucket and went to the kitchen for more hot water. Hofi had left a huge panful simmering. Beth poured it into the bucket, refilled the saucepan from the stream and set it once more on the burner. As she stepped down with the bucket, she almost collided with Rob.

'I bet you've taken the lot,' he accused, 'and me with sand and grit in places you wouldn't believe. We won't mention engine oil.'

'First come first served,' Beth retorted lightly. 'Just be grateful I've refilled the pan. It won't take long.'

'Too kind.' He bowed and made a sweeping gesture for her to pass. 'I suppose I'd better carry all that lovely hot water to your tent for you.'

'What a gracious offer,' Beth mocked. 'And to think I've been putting in good words on your behalf with a certain young lady.'

'You have?' Rob's face lit up. He snatched the bucket from her, doing a neat body-swerve as the water slopped over. 'Beth, you're a doll. For that, I'll even carry *you* back to your tent if you like. 'I'll crawl, I'll . . . '

'That won't be necessary,' she fended him off, laughing. 'Come on, I need my sleep, all this emotion is very tiring.'

He sobered instantly and glanced at her with compassion. 'Isn't it just.'

She drew a ragged breath, not speaking for several seconds. 'Is it so obvious?' she asked painfully.

He shook his head. 'Call it extra-sensory perception or maybe it's just that it takes one to know one. In the Land Rover I picked up odd vibes, but after Namaskard and your . . . ' he gestured towards her arm, '. . . accident, it got a little clearer. Sort of love-hate thing is it?'

Beth looked away. 'Sort of,' she murmured. She didn't want to even think about it. It was too complicated, too exhausting.

'Being totally selfish,' Rob went on, reading Beth's reaction correctly, 'I'm really only interested in me and whether you have managed to convince Gaynor what a terrific catch I am.'

'I've achieved the impossible and he wants miracles yet,' Beth muttered, rolling her eyes.

'Come on, Beth, put me out of my misery, what did you say? What did *she* say?'

Beth gave him a brief resumé of what Gaynor had told her, finishing up with what *she* had suggested. 'Give her time, Rob.'

'Time?' he groaned. 'I've only got a week.'

'On this expedition maybe,' Beth agreed. 'But if you find out you really do hit it off, you've got all the time in the world, haven't you?'

Rob set the bucket down outside the tent flap. Straightening up, he cupped Beth's face between his hands. 'You are a sweet and generous person, do you know that?'

'Go on,' Beth smiled at him, 'that's just a rumour put about by people I play Cupid for.'

'Thanks, Beth,' Rob said softly. 'I really do appreciate what you've done.' He leaned forward and planted a gentle kiss on her cheek.

Beth raised her hand and patted his sweatered shoulder. 'It's up to you now. Just one thing.'

'I know,' he cut in, his teeth gleaming in the fading light, 'keep my mouth shut.'

'You got it,' she laughed. 'Night, Rob.'

'Goodnight, Beth.' Giving her a final·hug he turned away and started back towards his tent.

Still smiling, Beth shook her head and bent to pick up the bucket. The sound of a pebble falling on to bare rock made her look round.

A few yards away, a black silhouette against the pink and gold sky, Allan stood, motionless.

Beth's heart lurched, thumping swiftly and uncomfortably against her ribs.

He must have seen Rob kiss her. Was that the reason for the anger she could feel emanating from him? It was tangible, a living force, and she flinched, taking an involuntary step backwards.

Jealous, Hofi had said. No, she couldn't believe that. She opened her mouth to explain, and shut it again. He wasn't jealous; that presupposed caring, and clearly all he felt for her was dislike. He was furious that she had disobeyed his instructions to stay away from Rob. Well, she owed him no explanations. Let him think what he liked.

Calmly and deliberately she turned her head away and lifted the tent flap.

'Stay where you are,' he commanded softly. 'I want to talk to you.'

'Well, I don't want to talk to you,' she retorted, reaching for the bucket.

'Good,' came the curt reply, 'because it's time you listened for a change. Now we can stay here and discuss private matters, with the risk of an audience, or we can take a walk. The choice is entirely yours.'

Beth swallowed. The whole situation was complicated enough without involving Rob and the Brennans. 'I—I'll get my jacket.'

She followed his tall figure up the sloping hillside past outcrops of dark, bare rock. Turning her collar up, she pushed her hands deep into her pockets. But the shivers goose-pimpling her skin were not a result of the chill night air, but of the apprehension churning inside her.

Eventually, just below the summit, he stopped. In the dusky glow of the midnight sun Beth could see the camp-site off to the left several hundred feet below, the only sign of life as far as the eye could see. The lingering aroma of coffee and cooking wafted past on the breeze and Beth realised with a moment's numbing fear that even if she screamed no one would hear her.

'Sit down,' Allan ordered.

There was no point in arguing. Beth sat, hugging her knees.

Allan lowered himself on to the ground beside her. He sat cross-legged, his fingers linked. He was not touching her, yet Beth's every nerve was alive to his nearness. Adrenalin surged through her veins, quickening her breathing, making her heart pound. All her muscles were drawn tight as she waited.

The silence stretched and Beth shuddered. The slight movement made Allan stir. He did not look at her as he spoke.

'It's time we sorted a few things out.'

Fighting to control the nervous tremor in her voice, she replied, 'I'd say it's all very clear.'

'Perhaps not,' was Allan's cryptic rejoinder.

It was too much for Beth. 'What's the point of all this?' she burst out. 'What right have you, of all people, to sit in judgement over me? Haven't you had your revenge?'

Slowly, Allan turned his head to look at her. 'Revenge?' His eyes burned with contempt, his mouth was bitter. 'Is that what you think this is all about?'

'Well? Isn't it?' she flared.

He did not reply immediately. 'There was a time,' Allan said softly, 'when I would have killed you.'

Beth felt all the colour drain from her face. 'You have no right——'

'No *right?*' he snarled. 'What has right to do with it? I loved you. You were life and breath to me. I thought, I believed, fool that I was, that you loved me.'

The air between them crackled with violence and tension, like heavy, inflammable vapour needing only a single spark to touch off a devastating explosion. His words tore like talons at her heart, and inwardly she bled.

'I *did* love you,' Beth cried, her face a mask of agony.

'Love?' His brief laugh was a raw, discordant sound. 'You don't know the meaning of the word. What was the crack you threw at me about the importance of honesty and trust?' His mouth curled in contempt. 'You hypocrite! Where was your trust, your honesty? You walked out on me without a word of explanation. I'd no idea of where you'd gone or why.'

'You had Shalana's letter,' Beth flung at him.

Allan looked startled, as though she had said something

completely irrelevant. He made an angry, dismissive gesture. 'What had that to do with *you?*'

She stared at him. He couldn't be serious. All the doubts about her own actions and behaviour that had surfaced since the beginning of the trip were extinguished in a blaze of anger and indignation. 'I'd have thought that was obvious. As for my staying, wouldn't it have been a little crowded with three of us? Besides,' she was weary, heartsick, 'I could not face hearing any more lies.'

'I have never lied to you.' His denial was firm and assured.

'No?' Beth almost choked, reliving the terrible moment when her whole world had shattered into a million fragments. 'I suppose it just slipped your memory that you already had a wife when you married me?'

'That is not true,' Allan contradicted flatly.

'You mean Shalana was just a figment of my imagination?' Beth demanded feverishly. 'I just dreamed this beautiful Indian woman standing in the doorway of your flat telling me I couldn't possibly by your wife because *she was?*'

Allan stared at her, his gaze narrowed and intense. She could sense his brain working at top speed. 'So,' he murmured, as though he had just received the answer to a question that had burned within him for a long, long time. 'Shalana was not my wife,' he said evenly.

'But she said . . .' Beth gazed at him in disbelief. Did he think she was mad, or stupid, or both? 'You expect me to believe that?'

His smile was bleak. 'I don't expect anything. I gave up *expecting* the day you walked out.'

Beth started to move, but Allan seized her hand, forcing her to remain exactly where she was. 'You're not running away again, Beth. This time you're going to hear the truth, whether you like it or not.'

Beth gasped and tried to pull away, but Allan merely tightened his grip.

'Be still, or I'll hurt you,' he snapped.

'More threats?' she taunted bitterly.

'Oh, no,' came the quiet, menacing reply. 'This one is a promise. You've cost me far more than you'll ever know. I'd enjoy the opportunity of redressing the balance.'

For several moments Beth glared at him, defiant, daring him to do his worst. But neither his cold gaze, nor the bruising pressure of his fingers showed any sign of faltering, and it was she who looked away.

'I got to know Shalana at university,' he began. 'We were in the same set. She was an intelligent girl and a serious student. After her finals she wanted to stay on and study for her Master's degree and her doctorate, but her family were pressuring her to return to India and an arranged marriage. When she resisted, her father threatened to cut off all financial support and have her deported as an illegal immigrant. Apparently, there was a lot of money and prestige involved in the arrangement.'

His grip had slackened somewhat, but his fingers were still warm and firm on hers. As Beth listened it was as though the ground on which she sat, so firm, so solid, had begun to shift, and cracks were opening up.

'Shani didn't know which way to turn,' Allan went on relentlessly. 'At first she wouldn't tell even us, her closest friends. Eventually we managed to persuade her. Jack and Ian had long-term steady girlfriends, and Richard was engaged. I was the only one unattached.'

The cracks widened, yawning open in front of Beth.

'I married Shani to give her British citizenship,' Allan said. 'It was a very quiet, businesslike affair, on a Monday at the beginning of December. It poured with rain. Not a bit like . . .' Even as he bit the words off, tension knotting his jaw, Beth's heart lurched as she recalled the day she and Allan had married in bright summer sunshine, with tears of laughter and happiness. There had been flowers, and singing and dancing, wonderful food and sparkling wine and even the local people had somehow got caught up in the infectious gaiety that had swept through the whole expedition party. It had been a joyous, magical day.

'Shalana and I were friends, not lovers,' Allan continued, his voice rasping. 'We never lived together either before or after the ceremony.' One corner of his mouth lifted in a sardonic grin. 'Shani had strong views about mixed marriages. She didn't approve of them. She cherished dreams of one day marrying an Indian of her own caste who would respect her intelligence. But she wanted the freedom to choose. As it happens, that was the way it worked out, and she has three handsome sons and a daughter. Our *marriage* was solely a legal convenience. Two months after the ceremony, as we had agreed, I began annulment proceedings.'

Beth couldn't have moved now, her legs would not have supported her. Head bent, she closed her eyes, her thoughts chaotic. She had been right, and yet so wrong. His voice echoed, cold and clear in her mind. *I have never lied to you.*

She tried to speak but no sound emerged from her parched throat. She swallowed painfully. 'Why didn't you tell me?' she whispered.

His face was granite-hard and each word fell like a hammer-blow. 'You didn't give me the chance.'

'No,' she muttered hoarsely, 'I meant why didn't you tell me before we were married?'

He pushed one hand through his hair. 'Since leaving university my life has been pretty full. I've worked all over the world in an absorbing, demanding job. A good turn for a friend that took a couple of days to plan and half an hour to carry out just wasn't important enough to remain at the front of my mind for the next eleven years. And once I'd met you——' His eyes flamed briefly. A wave of heat surged through Beth and her heart contracted.

'Once I'd met you,' he repeated flatly, 'I could barely think of anything else at all. I didn't tell you because I had quite simply forgotten all about it.'

Beth's head throbbed dully and she rubbed her temple with her free hand. 'Then why did Shalana come to the flat? Why was she so upset? And why did she tell me she was your wife?'

CHAPTER SIX

'BECAUSE,' Allan replied, 'at that moment she believed she was. And as she had a husband and four children, the idea was just as upsetting for her as it was for you. But of course you didn't think about that. You simply took the word of a distraught woman at face value and didn't even give her, *or me*, the chance to explain.' His tongue flayed her like a whip.

Beth flinched and, from beneath her lashes, watched him make a visible effort to control his bitter anger. When he spoke again his clipped tone was almost devoid of expression.

'She had seen a notice in the personal column of the paper that morning requesting that Allan Bryce and Shalana Prakesh-Bryce contact a certain firm of solicitors immediately. Shani recognised the firm as the one that had handled the annulment.

'As soon as her husband had gone to his surgery and she had taken her children to school, she began trying to contact me. We had lost touch and neither had the other's new address. After trying several Bryces in the phone book and getting nowhere, she decided to go to the solicitors herself. It seems the partner who dealt with our case had for some time been embezzling clients' money.

'Soon after Shani and I had sworn our affidavits and I had paid him in advance for what he assured us was a simple rubber-stamp job, he had absconded to Spain just one step ahead of the fraud squad. To cover his tracks he had left a very tangled web behind, and a lot of misfiled papers.

'It had been the discovery, by one of the other partners, of our papers, apparently incomplete, which had prompted the advertisement. They had written to our last known addresses, but the letters had never been sent on.'

Beth hung on to his every word.

'Shani had not told Akhil, her husband, about our *arrangement*, and if the annulment wasn't legal, it meant her present marriage was bigamous and her four children illegitimate. By the time she had managed to find out where I lived, and had arrived on the doorstep with a letter setting out the problem in case I wasn't at home, she was frantic with worry and had already convinced herself of the worst.'

Beth's eyes were wide and her hand shook as it crept up to cover her mouth. 'Oh, God,' she whispered, 'I didn't . . .'

Never in her wildest dreams had she imagined anything like this. 'If only . . . '

If only she had made Shalana wait, asked her to explain, invited her in until Allan got back. The last two years need never have happened. If only she had fought her childhood fears, refused to let them overwhelm her, forcing her to run rather than face a repeat of her mother's unhappiness. In the event, she had suffered far more than she would have believed possible. And it had all been totally unnecessary. *If only she had trusted him.*

'If only,' Allan repeated softly. 'That is one of the saddest phrases in the English language.' He released her hand. It felt cold and crushed.

Before Beth realised, he was on his feet. She was still dazed, still coming to terms with what she had learned.

Allan looked down at her. His face was expressionless, his eyes opaque, revealing nothing of his thoughts.

Beth had a sudden, horrifying premonition. He had forced her to listen to the full story. Now she knew the truth he was mentally washing his hand of her.

'The other,' he said quietly, confirming her fear, 'is *too late.*'

He turned to walk away. Beth scrambled stiffly to her feet.

'Allan . . . wait . . . please,' she cried. 'What happened? The annulment——'

He faced her once more and shrugged. 'As soon as I had read Shani's letter I collected her from her house and took her down to the solicitors' office. It was all sorted out within half an hour. A rubber-stamp job, just like the man said.'

Beth's skin crawled under his accusing gaze. Her mind filled with images of his returning home afterwards, waiting for her, prowling through the flat, perplexed, wondering where she was and why she hadn't left a note. Wondering when she'd be back. Then a few hours later, worried sick, he would have gone to their bedroom and, looking for some clue, opened the wardrobe and seen the empty rails. She swallowed painfully.

His gaze impaled her like a butterfly on a pin.

Her tongue snaked out. Her lips were so dry they had stuck to her teeth. 'Then . . .' she began unsteadily. 'I don't understand . . . if . . .' The words died away as realisation dawned. She caught her breath.

His smile was grim, humourless. 'That's right, Beth,' he grated. 'I'm still married. *And so are you.*' He started down the hillside, leaving her staring after him.

The following morning, after a restless night, Beth woke early. Leaving Gaynor still sleeping soundly, she dressed and crept out to wash in the icy stream. Relishing the solitude as the revelations of the previous day flooded back, she fetched her camera to capture the glorious colours and cloud effects in the morning sky.

Going through the motions of doing her job, as though this were just another day on the expedition, was her lifeline to normality. But it wasn't just another day. Once again her life had been turned upside down. She was not, as she had so firmly believed, the victim of lies, betrayal and bigamy, but a legally married woman. This complete reversal was too much to take in all at once.

Beth looked up at the sky. The streaks and veils of cloud were a visual gale warning, but though she saw them, they did not register. She was far more absorbed in the blend of pink and gold, primrose, silver and turquoise in the vast arcing sky. The distant hills appeared purple. And here, on the camp-site, each stunted blade of grass bowed beneath the weight of a single drop of dew hanging from its tip, reflecting the pastel shades of sunrise.

Walking to the lip of the grassy basin, Beth looked out across the sloping hillside, and froze. A short distance away, wearing a parka over his sweater against the morning chill, Allan was approaching.

'My husband,' Beth whispered to herself. The words sounded alien on her tongue yet at the same time kindled an uneasy excitement that disturbed her.

Head bent, as though looking inward at his own thoughts rather than outward at the wild and rugged scenery, he covered the ground with an easy, rhythmic stride.

Beth's instinct was to step back and avoid any contact, but something made her hesitate. In that fatal moment Allan looked up. For a split second he seemed to falter, but recovered instantly and continued towards her.

Apprehension started her heart thumping, but she could not back off. If she retreated now, he would still have to be faced tomorrow, and the next day, and the one after that. At least this morning they were alone, with no curious eyes to watch and wonder. She stood her ground.

She half expected him to walk straight past with merely a nod or the very briefest of greetings. Or would he make some cutting remark. *Or, ignore her completely.* She tensed, waiting, dreading.

He stopped about three feet from her, his eyes on a level

with hers as he stood just below the rim of the basin, yet far closer than a stranger would have.

'You're up early.' He spoke quietly, with no discernible inflection. 'Couldn't you sleep?'

Relief coursed through Beth. There was to be no scene, no verbal whiplash to flay her mentally. 'I didn't expect to,' she admitted. 'Yesterday was——' She stopped, swallowed, and attempted a smile. 'It seemed a very short night.' She looked up at the changing sky. 'Isn't it a beautiful morning?'

Frustration at her inability to capture the luminous reality of a scene interpreted as much by emotion as by eye imbued her voice with a wistfulness that caused Allan's features to tighten. A muscle jumped at the point of his jaw.

'They usually are out here.' He indicated her camera. 'Did you get some good shots?'

She made an impatient gesture, the irritation directed at herself. 'They are never good enough. Sometimes this is the most rewarding and maddening job in the world.'

'Still the perfectionist,' he observed.

Beth looked at him quickly, but neither his face nor his voice showed any trace of sarcasm. Nervous tension had dried her lips and she moistened them with the tip of her tongue, hiding the action by crouching to retie her bootlace. She placed the camera on the grass beside her foot.

They were metaphorically sniffing the air, circling one another like two wary animals, sensing vibrations which had no connection with the words they exchanged.

She straightened up. 'Have you been far?'

His grey eyes were slate-hard and cold as steel. 'To hell and back,' he replied softly.

Beth flinched. 'I—I meant this morning,' she stammered, trying desperately to keep everything normal and *safe*.

'This morning?' Allan pushed his hands into the pockets of his heavy parka. 'I suppose I covered a couple of miles.'

Beth's eyes widened. He must have been up at least an hour

before her. 'C—Couldn't you sleep?' she blurted. It was an innocuous enough question. He had asked her the same thing.

For a moment she thought he wasn't going to answer. He scanned the horizon through narrowed eyes. Beth watched his face, so familiar, yet that of a stranger, and felt a peculiar wrenching tug. She had been married to this man for two whole years, and had lived with him only two weeks.

As his gaze returned to her, Beth knew immediately something had changed. His eyes glittered and she could feel the simmering anger radiating from him.

With a soft gasp she stepped backwards, stumbling over her camera. His arm snaked out, his hand closing on her bruised forearm. Beth gave a little cry at the pain and wrenched free, cradling it against her breasts.

Allan's hands fastened on her shoulders. 'Why so anxious to leave?' he demanded softly. 'Here we are, after all this time, having a friendly, civilised chat, and all of a sudden you want to run away again. Why, Beth?'

She didn't answer. Her skin prickled and she began to shiver, sensing barely controlled violence in him.

He drew her inexorably towards him. She resisted with all her strength, pressing her hands against his chest. She could feel the strong thump of his heartbeat through the thick sweater. Her pulses clamoured.

'Don't, Allan, please.' She tried to hold her voice level, keeping her head slightly bent, avoiding his eyes, hiding the very real fear that threatened to overwhelm her.

Sliding one arm around her waist he pulled her hard against him. A muffled cry escaped her at the sudden movement and the shock of his once-adored body moulded to hers. Allan grasped her chin with his free hand, forcing her head up.

'Don't?' he mocked, his eyes ablaze with emotions she could not read. 'I didn't notice much protesting last night.'

She was confused. 'Last night? But we——' Then it dawned. *Rob.*

She returned his gaze, her fear turning to anger. 'Jealous?' she challenged, fiercely glad to be able to turn the tables on him.

Allan laughed softly. 'Of a boy trying to do a man's job?'

Beth made a vain attempt to ignore what was happening. A slow, gentle warmth radiated outwards from the centre of her body. Soothing, beguiling, it tempted her to stop fighting, to forget everything but this moment.

Why not let her head nestle in the angle of his neck and shoulder the way it used to? Why not slide her hands around the lithe, hard-muscled body and, for the first time in two long, empty years, relax in a man's arms? And who better than this man? Wasn't it he who had, with such patience and tenderness, transformed her from an inexperienced girl into a sensual, fulfilled woman?

She sensed his tension, felt his warm breath on her cheek. His fingers strayed along her jaw, caressing her ear, her neck. She shivered and swallowed convulsively. *Allan, my husband.*

'Remember, Beth?' he whispered, lowering his head.

Unable to help herself, she closed her eyes. His lips were warm and infinitely gentle against her skin.

'Remember,' he repeated hoarsely, a command, not a question. A shudder ran through him. His arm tightened, crushing the breath out of her. His tongue parted her lips, sending tiny white-hot flames along her nerves. Her fingers clenched on his sweater and she trembled against him. As his kiss deepened, demanding response, her resistance crumbled.

With paralysing suddenness he thrust her away. *'No.'* The word was wrenched from his throat, a harsh rejection.

Allan Bryce gazed at the young woman hanging limply in his punishing grip. Her piquant face was flushed, her eyes heavy-lidded, and her mouth soft and rosy, moist from his kiss. Her vulnerability tore at him. He wanted to kill her, and he wanted . . . he wanted . . . He battled against the rising tide of desire. He had intended to arouse her, to use her with contempt, and in mocking the act of love, cauterise the wounds of his own suffering. But the plan, so clear and simple, had backfired, for he could not remain aloof. He had loved her as he had loved no other woman. She had captured his heart and soul as well as delighting his body. *And she had left him without a word.* Shaken by the violence of his own feelings, the mixture of hatred and longing, he let her go, thrusting his hands into his pockets.

Bewildererd, still caught up in the physical and emotional turmoil he had unleashed, Beth swayed towards him.

Slowly, deliberately, Allan wiped his mouth with the back of his hand.

The gesture had the same effect on Beth as a slap across the face. The shock made her dizzy. She couldn't breathe.

'Damn you,' Allan whispered and wheeling round, he strode away across the camp-site to the tent he shared with Rob.

Beth turned her back on the little cluster of tents. She felt sick and weak. Tears of rage and shame and something more, something she could not identify, spilled down her cheeks. Gulping back sobs, she dashed them away, using her fingers, then her palms. 'Bastard, *bastard,*' she choked.

On the clear, still air she heard Gaynor yawn and stretch. Eugene coughed and Lucille muttered. The camp was stirring. Picking up her camera, Beth went down to the stream and bathed her hot face in the crystal water.

They were on the road again by nine. Breakfast, consisting of cereal, yoghurt, rolls and jam, and a mug of tea or coffee, had been a hastily consumed meal, with little of the relaxed atmosphere of the previous evening.

Undercurrents of anticipation and excitement at what new discoveries this next stage of the journey might bring showed in the speed of preparation for striking camp.

While Gaynor helped Hofi wash up and secure everything in the kitchen trailer ready for travelling, Beth completed Gaynor's packing, which involved collecting items from every corner of the tent, and her own, then began dismantling the tent.

When Rob breezed over offering to help, as his own gear was all packed and loaded, Beth immediately declined. 'I expect Allan has a job in mind for you.' She smiled at him to take the sting out of the abrupt refusal. She had no intention of giving Allan Bryce any more ammunition to fire at her. In any case it wasn't fair to involve Rob in a situation he knew nothing about and she could not explain.

'He has,' Rob agreed. Bending down, he folded the collapsed tent into a neat oblong. 'This is it.'

Beth stared at him in disbelief. 'He sent you to help me?'

Rob nodded. 'Why so surprised? Gaynor's helping Hofi, so she's not here to do her share. And much as I adore her, I'm not blind to the fact that she's dreadfully untidy which makes twice as much work for you. Neither has she any experience of camping, so she'll be more hindrance than help when it comes to pitching the tent or taking it down. I mentioned this to Allan and he suggested I gave you a hand.'

'I can manage, if there's something else you want to do,' Beth said quickly. 'I don't mind, honestly.' It was the truth. She preferred working alone, especially this morning. She was still deeply shaken by what had happened.

It wasn't just the shock of Allan kissing her, though that had been the very last thing she had expected. But her own response, the hungry yearning that had overridden two years of grief and the rebuilding of a shattered life, as though *nothing* mattered but being back in his arms, she would not easily forgive herself for that.

The ultimate degradation had been Allan's gesture of wiping the touch and taste of her kiss from his mouth. Even as she recalled it, shame scalded her.

'Well, whether you mind or not,' Rob carried on neatly rolling the tent, 'Sir sent me to help and I, for one, do not feel inclined to argue. He's on a very short fuse this morning. He even snapped at Gunnar.'

Beth looked up from the poles she was taking apart. 'What for?'

Rob shrugged. 'Who knows? Gunnar certainly didn't. I think he asked if Allan knew how your arm was. How is it, by the way?'

Beth recalled how Allan had seized it. With her shirt-sleeve and sweater covering the bandage there had been no visible sign to remind him and she had seen perplexity then realisation flit across his hard features when she gasped at the pain and snatched it free. But he had not apologised. Perhaps he felt she deserved it. After all it was entirely her own fault.

'It's OK. Still a bit sore, but that's only to be expected.' She handed him the poles and held the canvas bag open for him to pack in the rolled-up tent, the poles, pegs and coiled guy-ropes. Then while he steadied it, she pulled the cord tight and tied it.

Rob lowered his voice. 'Did you know Gaynor's *dear* mother is trying to cut me out and push Gaynor under Allan's nose as a prospective bride?'

'*What?*' Beth frowned. Hadn't Gaynor told her mother about Rob's interest in her? Or was Lucille simply ignoring her daughter, determined to do what *she* had decided was best, regardless of Gaynor's feelings in the matter?

'You know, under that pink, fluffy hair and sweet Taxas charm beats a heart of pure flint,' Rob muttered.

'Don't let it worry you,' Beth comforted him. 'I think Lucille is in for a shock. Gaynor isn't her mother's daughter for nothing. Lucille can scheme and dream to her heart's content, but I've an idea Gaynor has other plans, if a certain person not a million miles from here will have a bit of faith in himself.'

Hope washed across Rob's face. 'Has Gaynor been talking about me?'

Beth tilted her head to one side. 'I believe your name has cropped up in conversation once or twice.'

'And I'm in with a chance? Beth,' Rob grinned delightedly and, tucking the tent under one arm scooped up Gaynor's case with the other, 'if I wasn't promised to another, I'd marry you.'

Masking a stab of grief, Beth pretended horror. 'Don't you threaten me.' Then picking up her suitcase and cameras, she followed him to the vehicles.

Within minutes the loading was finished. Allan jumped down, and Rob turned from a pink-cheeked Gaynor to ask him if he had any objections to Beth changing places and moving into the front seat.

Beth had studiously avoided Allan since his muttered curse and abrupt departure. But Rob's wish to alter the arrangements directly affected her, and so it was to Allan that her gaze automatically flew.

He was watching her, his face an inscrutable mask. She waited for the refusal she was certain would come, salvaging the remains of her pride to keep her head high.

'Do *you* have any objections?' he enquired in a voice devoid of expression.

Beth caught the inside of her lip between her teeth, surprised not only by the question, but that he should ask it. The very last thing she wanted was to sit beside him. Yet, knowing how much it meant to Rob, how could she refuse? Her gaze slid towards the door. Rob's fingers linked with Gaynor's while Lucille looked on in obvious disapproval.

'No,' Beth said, and flashing her a wide grin and a wink, Rob opened the door for Gaynor and climbed in beside her.

'Right, let's get moving,' Allan shouted and Beth settled herself in the front seat, stowed her camera case at her feet and slammed the door. At least she didn't have to spend the morning avoiding the driving-mirror.

Yet, as they left the grassy basin and followed the narrow, sandy track into the desert through dunes of black gravel, though Beth stared out of the window, keeping her head averted, she could not help but be aware of the man beside her.

He had discarded his parka and pushed the sleeves of his sweater half-way up his forearms. His strong, brown hand moved frequently from wheel to gear lever and back as he skilfully guided the vehicle around large boulders without losing speed.

Over a period of time, the passage of vehicles over the track had pushed the gravel into ridges on either side and down the middle. Driving in the ruts meant jolting and vibration. But when, in an effort to ease this, Allan drove on the gravel, the wheel lost traction and spun without gripping, and the engine screamed.

After almost two hours' travelling, Beth was aching and weary. Then they came to a lava field. As Allan followed Gunnar along the track running beside the plates of bare flat rock, Rob leaned forward. But before he could speak the radio crackled.

Allan answered and Gunnar's voice announced that Eugene wanted photographs, long shots and close-ups. Allan made a brief acknowledgement and pulled up close behind Gunnar.

Beth took both cameras out of their case, slung them round her neck and opened the door. Allan was already out and had the back door open.

'You'll need this,' he said as she passed and handed her her padded anorak.

He was right. The stiff breeze had a keen edge that struck through her shirt and sweater, bringing her skin up in goose-pimples. 'Thank you,' Beth murmured politely and began walking away as she put it on. This was yet another Allan and she was wary, suspicious. When would he deliver the next blow? Was he honing another shaft to deadly perfection, ready to strike again?

'Gee, why is it so cold?' Gaynor's husky voice carried towards Beth.

'The wind is coming off the glacier,' Rob explained.

'But it's at least a couple of days before we reach it.' Gaynor hugged the soft mink collar of her leather jacket around her ears. 'I mean that's *miles.*'

'There is more ice on Vatnajökull than in the whole of Europe,' Allan replied and Beth detected beneath his impatience a note of concern. 'We could have frost tonight and a snowstorm before that.'

Beth raised the Nikon and got a panoramic view of the lava field and the huge dunes and ridges of black gravel that bordered it. Above the southern horizon, a thick bank of grey cloud, dappled coppery-bronze by the low sun, was advancing across the streaked sky. She took a second closer shot of the lava blocks which showed the rays of the sun glancing off them, turning them to slabs of ebony and gold. The crevices between the blocks were filled with fine black sand.

Switching cameras, Beth lay on her stomach to capture the varying textures of the lava, pumice and ash that edged the field.

Eugene hurried over as Beth stood up and brushed herself down. 'You sure you got enough? Just take your time. I got some great samples of this here rock and sand. Whaddya say to a couple more shots?'

Beth caught Allan's slight frown. It was clear they had stopped long enough. Having taken all the photographs she wanted, Beth had no wish to antagonise him just for the sake of it. He had proved himself too powerful and damaging an opponent. 'I've got quite a few, Eugene. They're all good. We'll see more lava formations further on.' She flicked a glance at Allan and was rewarded with an almost imperceptible nod. 'Unless I'm careful I could run out of film before we reach the glacier. I won't miss anything important, I promise. I think Allan wants to get moving again. The weather doesn't look too good and this isn't a very hospitable place to be stranded.'

'Too right,' Eugene agreed at once, and scurried away.

'OK, folks,' Allan shouted, 'let's move on.'

As Beth reached the Land Rover and turned the door handle, she saw Hofi and Gunnar standing a little to one side of their vehicle.

Looking up, Hofi saw Beth and waved.

'All right?' Beth shouted. That could mean anything, she reasoned. It wasn't betraying a confidence.

'Fine,' came the bright reply and, with another quick wave, Hofi dived into the Land Rover.

Gunnar gave a brief shrug and lumbered round to the driving-seat, shaking his head.

Rob and Gaynor dashed up, pink-cheeked and laughing, and scrambled in, followed by Allan. Moments later they were once more on their way.

After following the edge of the lava field for some distance, the track then turned and went straight through it. The Land Rover lurched and jolted over plates of bare rock, the track made more tortuous by twists and turns to avoid taller blocks of lava.

Beth tried to brace herself, hanging on to the door and the seat in an attempt to stop herself being thrown against the metal on one side or Allan on the other. She had loosened the seat-belt, unable to bear its constriction. But now her insides felt like jelly and her head had begun to throb.

Feeling a gentle tap on her shoulder she roused herself and looked round.

'Are you OK?' Gaynor mouthed.

Beth darted a quick glance at Allan's hard profile. She felt rotten but did not dare admit it. She had insisted on coming though Allan clearly had not wanted her to. The incident at Namaskard had put one huge black mark against her already. In fact it was probably reaction to the fright, to seeing Allan again, and to the shattering discovery that they were still married that was making her feel so dreadful.

With an effort she nodded. 'How about you?'

As Allan changed gear yet again and they swayed around another huge boulder in their path, Gaynor pulled a face.

Allan's glance flicked to the mirror. 'What's the matter?' he shouted above the engine noise.

Gaynor leaned forward. 'I don't feel so good.'

He half turned his head, keeping his eyes on the track. 'We'll be through this and into desert again soon. Can you hang on a bit longer?'

Gaynor hesitated then nodded.

'Have a go at Granny's cologne,' Allan suggested.

'Why didn't I think of that?' Rob put his arm round Gaynor's shoulders, held her handbag while she rummaged, then drew her back against him as she stroked cologne on to her wrists and temples.

Its pungent scent filled the air, and Beth felt her stomach contract. *Oh, no!* She grabbed Allan's arm. 'I'm sorry,' she gasped, her head spinning. 'You must stop, *now.*'

Allan slammed on the brakes but even before the vehicle had skidded to a halt, Beth was out of the door and stumbling towards the privacy of some rocks.

She hunched there, eyes closed, her breathing shallow, cold perspiration dewing her face, as she fought the nausea that had threatened to overwhelm her.

Her misery was complete. Allan would verbally tear her to pieces. She saw yet again that terrible look in his eyes as he thrust her away, wiping her kiss from his mouth with the back of his hand.

'Beth?' Gaynor's voice, some distance away, broke into her thoughts.

'I'm OK,' Beth called back, 'I'll be with you in a minute.' She put her hands over her face and sucked in deep steadying breaths. She couldn't stay here. No doubt Allan was already furious. The longer she held everyone up, the madder he would get. And he would make her pay. She had no doubt of it.

A cool, wet cloth was wiped gently across the back of her neck and, as she lowered her hands, a cupful of cold water was placed in them.

'Thanks,' Gay——' she began, then, eyes widening, her head flew up, and she found herself gazing into Allan's stern face.

She felt her skin tighten and every muscle grew tense as she waited for his anger to break over her.

He crouched in front of her and guided the cup to her lips. His eyes never left hers as she swallowed, once, twice, The water calmed her stomach, soothed her dry throat. He lowered the cup and handed her the cloth.

'Wipe your face,' he said quietly.

Beth did as she was told, and felt strength gradually returning to her limbs. 'I—I'm all right now,' she said, lifting her head. 'Really. We can go on as soon as you like. I—I'm sorry I held everyone up.' She shrugged helplessness. 'I've *never* —it's—I don't know why——' Her hand rose and fell as she stammered, 'I've never been car-sick before. I feel such a fool.'

'There's no need,' Allan replied evenly. 'Gaynor and Hofi are both queasy as well. In any case, I don't think yours is motion-sickness.'

Beth raised her eyes to his.

'You've had one or two shocks this past couple of days.' His voice was calm and expressionless, but his eyes as they bored into hers seemed to be searching. For what? Beth wondered dazedly.

Suddenly he stood up, towering over her, a stranger once more. 'If you're sure you're all right, will you go and see to Hofi? She's been asking for you.'

'Yes, of course.'

Allan was already walking away. Beth stared after him. Why had he come himself? Why hadn't he sent one of the others with the damp cloth and drink of water?

She picked her way back through the rocks to the track. Rob

was walking an ashen-faced Gaynor up and down, fending off
a clearly irritated Lucille. 'Hofi?' she asked as he threw her a
sympathetic grin.

He pointed down the track. 'Cuppa?'

'You'll go to Heaven for that,' Beth smiled gratefully, over
her shoulder.

She found Hofi, hunched over as she had been, behind a
rock. 'It's all right,' she said quickly as Hofi jumped. 'It's only
me.'

'Oh, Beth,' Hofi groaned. 'I did not think it would be like
this.'

'I want the truth.' Beth was quiet but firm. 'What's wrong?
You haven't been yourself since I arrived. You can't go on
pretending everything is fine when it so obviously isn't.
Gunnar is worried, *I'm* worried.'

Hofi rolled her head against the rock and looked up at Beth.
'Nothing is *wrong,*' she said, trying to suppress a smile. Then
before Beth could argue, she whispered, 'I think I am having a
baby.'

'Oh, Hofi,' Beth squeezed her friend's hand. 'I'm so happy
for you.' There was a huge lump in her throat. Once, a long
time ago, she had thought about babies. She had not wished
for one right away. She hadn't wanted to share Allan with
anyone for a few years, not even a child born of their love. But,
because of her fear, in place of all the plans, all the tomorrows,
there had been two long years of bitterness, loneliness, and an
aching void she had tried hard and unsuccesfully to fill with
work.

Her face must have mirrored her thoughts for Hofi touched
her hand, her expression sympathetic. 'Beth——' she began,
but Beth cut her off.

'Come on,' she said, brisk and cheerful, for Hofi's pity
would undo her completely, 'we'd better get back. Rob's
making some tea. I'm sure you'll feel fine again——'

'You English,' Hofi teased, 'you think the answer to

everything is a cup of tea.'

Beth managed a wry smile. 'It might not be the answer, but it does give one time to gather a few wits.'

'Beth.' Hofi hung back, her expression suddenly serious. 'Don't tell Gunnar about the baby.

'Of course not.' Beth was surprised at her friend. '*You* must do that.'

'But not yet. Not until we get home.'

Beth frowned. 'Hofi, you can't wait that long. What if you're sick again? Gunnar is concerned about you already. He'll be worried to death if this goes on and you *don't* tell him.'

'Please, Beth.' Hofi looked strained. 'You say nothing. I will say, when time is right, when I am sure . . . ' Her voice tailed off and her chin quivered.

Suddenly Beth understood. 'You're afraid of another disappointment?'

Hofi nodded and looked down at her fingers. She glanced up at Beth with a watery grin. 'Mind, the other times it was never like this, never the——' She grimaced and rubbed her stomach.

Putting an arm around her, Beth squeezed Hofi's shoulders. 'Please tell him, Hofi. Don't shut him out. Gunnar loves you. He will want to share it all, the joy and pain; the happiness and the sorrow.'

'You will say nothing?' Hofi insisted.

Beth hesitated then shrugged. 'I won't say a word.'

Allan was prising a stone from one of the tyres, but everyone else was gathered near the kitchen trailer. Gaynor, completely recovered, was handing out cups of tea and coffee and sandwiches.

Catching sight of Hofi and Beth, she immediately made a joke about her own queasiness and how they had flung her in at the deep end of pioneer life.

Gunnar hugged his wife and kissed her several times, patently relieved to see her all right once more. Watching them, Beth's sense of loss was more than she could bear and she turned away, only to glimpse Allan's inscrutable face. Without her noticing, he had joined the group. Lucille had edged over to him and, with an innocent expression on her plump face, was talking quietly and insistently to him.

Allan stood at right angles to her, his head inclined in her direction. But it was at Beth that he looked, his gaze burning in its intensity, a combination of yearning and hatred that dried her mouth.

She started violently as Gaynor spoke, her pulse hammering in her throat. That gaze would haunt her.

'Can I get you something, Beth? Allan decided we should eat now, just a scratch meal, to save having to stop again,' she pulled a face, 'stomachs permitting. I made some sandwiches, cold meat and pickle.'

Rob tried to slide his arm around her. Stifling a giggle, Gaynor knocked it away in a gesture that quite obviously was not meant to be taken seriously.

'I think you've both earned yourselves a break.' Beth made an effort to smile, while her heart ached with envy for both Gaynor and Hofi. 'I'll see to my own lunch.'

'You're a pal,' Gaynor grinned.

'I'll second that.' Rob winked at her as Gaynor jumped down into his waiting arms to Lucille's tight-lipped disapproval.

As Beth climbed into the trailer, Eugene demanded to know where Rob and Gaynor were going.

'To look at the lava tunnels,' Rob replied at once. 'Would you care to join us?'

'No.' Eugene shook his grizzled head. 'I've seen 'em already.' He turned away and was almost bowled over by an irate Lucille who, in fierce whispers, vented the full force of her irritation on him.

With a wry grin Beth poured herself some tea. Cupping the mug in both hands she leaned back against the work-top. She didn't feel hungry, but knew she ought to eat something.

The light from the doorway was blocked by Allan's tall figure as he stepped, head bent, into the trailer. Cramped before, it now seemed claustrophobic and Beth backed into a corner.

Seeming oblivious of her, Allan made himself a cup of coffee, then took a sandwich from the plate. Beth's unease turned to antagonism. Why didn't he say something? Was he simply going to ignore her? Pretend she wasn't there?

As if reading her thoughts, he turned, coffee in one hand, sandwich in the other and, stationing himself between her and the door, leaned one hip against the work-top.

'Tell me what's wrong with Hofi.'

Beth had expected irritation, even downright anger at the delay, so the concern in Allan's voice took her by surprise. It must have shown on her face for his features tightened.

'They're my closest friends,' he rasped. 'I want to know and I want the truth.'

Beth twisted the mug around between her fingers, torn by indecision. She had given Hofi her word. She glanced sideways at Allan. 'Hofi is *my* best friend,' she countered.

Allan guessed at once. 'And she's asked you not to say anything?'

Beth nodded unhappily.

'Look, as leader, the responsibility for everyone's safety is mine.' Allan stated the fact quietly.

'I *know*,' Beth acknowledged and looked up at him again. 'There's nothing *wrong*. I mean she's not *ill*, it's—she——' Beth shook her head.

Allan's eyes narrowed, then enlightenment dawned. 'She's pregnant?'

Beth nodded. 'And terrified that if she tells Gunnar before it's officially confirmed by the doctor, she'll lose it. I know it sounds ridiculous, but emotionally she's very vulnerable. Allan, she made me promise not to tell Gunnar,' Beth said, her reserve abandoned, her fear of him forgotten, as all her thoughts centred on Hofi's dilemma. 'They've wanted this baby for so long. There have been several false alarms during the past few years. That's why she's terrified to believe it's really happening at last. It's the only way she can handle the possibility of yet another disappointment.'

'And she's trying to carry on as normal?'

Beth shrugged. 'That's what she wants. But I don't see how she can.'

'She can't.' Allan was brusque. 'It's out of the question. I'll make arrangements to have her airlifted out when we reach the strip at Herdubreidarlindar. Gaynor can take over the cooking, it will give her a chance to be useful as well as decorative.'

Beth turned away, carefully placing her empty mug on the work-top, fighting the needle of jealousy she knew was ridiculous. Gaynor *was* beautiful. She was also funny and sweet and Rob adored her and now Allan was admitting he found her attractive, and life was *bloody*.

'Of course,' she heard the strain in her voice, 'nothing must upset the expedition.'

Allan slammed down his mug, tossed aside the half-eaten sandwich, and caught Beth's shoulders, wrenching her round to face him, ignoring her gasp. 'To hell with the expedition,' he grated. 'Hofi has already taken too many risks. This is Gunnar's baby too. And he has to be told. He has a *right* to know what's going on, for God's sake. Do you think that I——? If *we* had——? He broke off, letting her go, and turned his back, gripping the door surround with both hands, his head bent. 'Tell Hofi I forced you to break your promise,' he said harshly. 'Tell her to blame me.' Without another word he disappeared from the trailer.

Beth rubbed her upper arms, still feeling his strong fingers. *If we had* . . . As though a curtain had been pulled aside, Beth realised for the first time just how much he had suffered. Not mere anger or hurt pride, but a grievous sense of loss, *exactly* like hers. She blinked hard to banish the scalding tears behind her eyelids. 'Oh, Allan,' she whispered, 'will you ever be able to forgive me?'

She emerged from the trailer to see Allan, Hofi and Gunnar talking quietly together. Allan was determined, Hofi reluctant, and Gunnar obviously confused. Then Hofi drew her husband's head down and whispered in his ear.

Gunnar's expression changed from uncertainty to stunned disbelief, then exultation. He gave a great whoop of delight, scooped Hofi up in his arms as if she were weightless, and whirled her round, raining kisses on every part of her face he could reach. 'A baby!' he bellowed, as first Lucille and Eugene, then Rob and Gaynor came running to see what was wrong. 'I am going to have a baby!'

CHAPTER SEVEN

BY mid-afternoon they had left the lava field behind, emerging into sandy desert. Below the thick blanket which had blotted out the sun, more clouds, with torn, ragged edges, raced across the sky, driven by the wind. Gusting to gale force, it buffeted the Land Rover and Gaynor voiced Beth's own feelings when she observed uneasily, 'Gee, it sure is wild out here.'

There was not a single sign of life, no birds, no plants, not even a blade of grass, on the barren land around them.

Beth fingered the camera slung from her neck, unconsciously seeking reassurance. The combination of brooding sky and barren landscape was alien and threatening. Even the light had an eerie quality.

Her gaze was drawn to Allan's hard profile. They had to talk. This time it would be she who explained. Once he knew about her father, surely he would understand why she had . . . *run away*. God, what a cowardly fool she had been. She had talked of love, and thought only of herself. She turned her head quickly to look out of the side window.

But what she saw made her eyes widen, and instinctively she gripped Allan's bare forearm. 'What's that?' she cried, pointing at the swirling black cloud that seemed to reach from the angry sky to the ground.

Leaning forward, Allan peered out of her window, muttered a vicious expletive and slammed on the brakes, hurling them all forward against their seat-belts. 'Sandstorm,' came the curt reply.

As he grabbed the microphone to warn Gunnar who was still speeding across the flat desert surface, Beth hit the release catch, opened her door, and jumped out.

The wind tore at her hair and she slitted her eyes as sand and grit stung her face and hands. Raising the camera she pressed the shutter button, taking shot after shot as the towering curtain bore down on them with the speed of an express train.

Half turning, she snapped Gunnar's Land Rover, a hundred yards ahead, just as a freak ray of sunlight broke through, illuminating the cream paintwork so that it stood out clearly against the black desert sand and the grey and bronze clouds.

'Beth! Get in here!' Allan roared.

'Coming,' she called and after one last picture, dived back in, clipping the lens cap on. As she slammed the door it was as if a giant hand thumped the side of the Land Rover, rocking it on its chassis.

Then day became night and the air was filled with a high-pitched whistling and hissing as grit and sand blasted against glass and metal.

Gaynor shrieked in panic and through the noise Beth heard Rob soothing her. She visualised them snuggling close and her envy stabbed like a knife.

Holding the camera against her with one hand, her anorak unzipped, Beth clutched the seat with the other, rigid with alarm, as the wind battered the vehicle, trying, it seemed, to lift it off the ground.

Her mind accepted what was happening, but as the shrill keening gnawed at her senses and the air grew thick with dust, her heart thudded sickeningly and her nerves were stretched taut. The darkness pressed down like a weight.

She felt Allan move. He was shutting the ventilators. He turned to her. 'Check your window,' he ordered. 'Make sure it is shut tight.'

The grit was in her nose and mouth. She was finding it

difficult to breathe. She tried to swallow but the dust had dried in her throat. She couldn't see him. She couldn't see anything. The wind was a malevolent force, screaming as it tried to reach them.

'Beth,' he repeated, more forcefully this time, 'your window.'

She let go of the camera and it swung against her chest as she fumbled for the handle. The Land Rover bucked and heaved as the wind slammed against it once more. Beth gasped, and coughed.

Allan lunged across in front of her. He tightened the handle and the shrill whistling lessened a fraction. He started to move back. Letting go of the seat, Beth grabbed his hand and clung to it. The move was totally unpremeditated, barely conscious, an instinctive reaching out in fear for the comfort of another human being.

For an instant Allan did not respond, then his fingers closed over hers and he gently rubbed her knuckles with his thumb.

Almost at once some of the fear left her. Sliding his free arm along the back of the seat, Allan moved closer so that their thighs touched and her shoulder pressed against his chest. Beth let out a shaky sigh.

His mouth was close to her ear. He only needed to raise his voice slightly to be heard above the din. 'You should have a prize-winner if those pictures come out.'

She nodded. 'If is right.' Her voice was cracked and tremulous, but at least the horrible visions of the Land Rover turning over and trapping them all had receded. 'The camera is probably full of dust. Still, it was worth a try. Not that I had much time to think,' she laughed unsteadily. 'I was on automatic.'

His hand was warm and firm. It comforted and strengthened her. She could feel his body-warmth through her thigh and shoulder. From behind her came rustling and

soft murmurs. Aware of their significance, she tried to
ignore the sounds. But memories of the first kiss she had
shared with Allan haunted her, filling her with a yearning
that was almost too painful to bear. And in that moment she
knew. Like lightning splitting the darkness, the truth
dazzled and shocked her. She still loved him.

Soft as a breath, his lips brushed her cheek, strangely
tentative, almost as if he was drawn to her against his will.

Beth's heart flipped over, its beat thundering in her ears,
drowning every other sound. She moved, not away, but
towards him. She felt his face close, so close, and as she
rested her head on his arm, he laid his cheek against hers.
Amid the noise and stress it was a moment of utter peace.

Raising his head, his mouth, warm and infinitely gentle,
covered hers. His hand tightened for an instant, then
released hers. Cupping her face, he stroked her neck with
his fingertips.

Beth trembled. She had forgotten the potency of his
touch. It was new, yet achingly, gloriously familiar.

He made a soft sound deep in his throat, and her mouth
opened like a flower beneath his. She felt his swift indrawn
breath and buried her fingers in his hair, revelling in its
thickness and silky texture. He pushed her jacket aside,
seeking the soft curve of her breast. Unable to help herself,
responding to a need as old as time, Beth arched towards
him. His hand slid to her lower back and, roughly, he
pulled her close.

The camera was a sudden, uncomfortable barrier. They
broke apart, both reaching for it, their breathing quick,
urgent. But as Allan lifted the strap from around her neck,
the blackness paled.

For an instant neither moved. In the gloom his eyes had a
fierce, hungry glitter that sent a shaft of exquisite weakness
through the pit of Beth's stomach, making her catch her
breath. Then, straightening up, he let the strap fall and

turned away.

Eyes lowered, cheeks flaming, she brushed grit from her hair and clothes, and carefully wiped the dust off her camera, acutely conscious of the man beside her and of the slow, smouldering flame he had ignited.

As suddenly as it had arrived, the sandstorm departed. Beth blinked and daylight returned, filtering dimly through the thick layer of dust caking the windows.

With more rustling, whispers, and a stifled giggle, Rob and Gaynor untangled themselves.

'Wow!' Gaynor laughed breathlessly, tugging at her jacket, 'that really was something.'

'One does one's best,' Rob said, affecting modesty as he examined his fingernails.

Scarlet, Gaynor elbowed him in the ribs. 'I meant the sandstorm,' she spluttered.

'What do you think *I* meant?' he demanded, all pained innocence. 'We arranged that sandstorm just for you. All part of the service. Safaris with a smile. Sandstorms our speciality.' He raised his voice. 'Isn't that so, Beth?'

'Don't you drag me into it,' she grinned over her shoulder. 'I'm not a party to management decisions. Just one of the workers, that's me.'

Rob made a retort, but she smiled vaguely and swivelled round in her seat, not really listening.

Allen checked that all was well with Gunnar's party, then, using a soft cloth to avoid scratching the glass, he wiped the dust and grit from the windows, and they resumed their journey.

Beth stared out at the desert, but saw nothing.

She might still love Allan, but what of him? What did he feel for her? Except when circumstances had literally thrown them together, his manner towards her had shown no sign of softening.

Was that so surprising? He had trusted her once, and she

had betrayed that trust. Shadows from the past had proved stronger than her love for him. How could she blame him for being reluctant to commit himself again? Somehow she had to win back his trust and prove herself worthy of his love.

But did she have the courage? Only yesterday he had wiped her kiss from his mouth as though her very touch was contaminating. And he had damned her while he did so. Yet a few moments ago it had been so different. For those few magical seconds all the misery and suffering of the past two years was forgotten as their need for one another transcended everything else.

But when, no longer touching her, he turned away, it seemed somehow as though he had moved far beyond her reach.

Beth was afraid. She was on a slippery slope with nothing to slow her down and no idea where she was heading.

The Land Rover stopped with a slight jolt, jerking her back to the present. Allan was already out. He had left his door wide open and the breeze swirled the fine dust into the air once more. Before them was a cloudy, fast-flowing river.

Grabbing her camera case, Beth jumped out, pushing her door back as far as it would go, hoping the through draught would blow the dust away and clear the air. Rob and Gaynor clambered out behind her.

Gunnar had the bonnet of his Land Rover up. A few yards from the group, Beth opened her case, removed the film from the Nikon and popped it into the bag with the others ready for processing. Then, swiftly and expertly, she cleaned and reloaded the camera.

Hearing Eugene asking if something was wrong, Beth glanced up to see him peering under the bonnet. Hofi passed Gunnar a plastic bag and a rubber band as he handed her an aerosol can. 'It is water repellent,' she explained to Eugene. 'We have to cross the river. Gunnar will fasten the bag over the distributor and the water will not short the electrics. We hope,' she added, raising crossed fingers.

Shutting the metal case, Beth hurriedly put it back on her seat, then returned to the river bank and began taking pictures.

Allan had fetched a pair of waders and a coil of rope from the back of Gunnar's Land Rover. The waders came up to his thighs.

'What's he doing that for?' Gaynor asked as Gunnar tied one end of the coiled rope to the heavy metal bar bolted in front of the radiator then passed the rest back to Allan

'He's going to tow the Land Rover across,' Rob answered, straight-faced.

Gaynor gazed up at him. 'Really?'

'Oh, yes,' Rob nodded. 'You watch, any minute now he'll put the rope between his teeth and start pulling.'

Hofi and Beth glanced at one another, smothering grins while Gaynor watched Allan expectantly. Rob cleared his throat to muffle a snorting laugh and Gaynor, realising he was teasing, whirled round with a shriek and pummelled him. 'You keep doing that and I keep falling for it!' she accused him.

He yelped and grabbed her, pinning her arms to her sides, then kissed her nose. 'I shall have to find a way of curbing your tendency to violence,' he tutted, shaking his head.

'Oh, yeah?' she challenged, her eyes sparkling. 'You and the Dallas Cowboys?'

With her piled-up hair dishevelled and her face bare of make-up, Gaynor had never looked happier or more beautiful. Beth snapped her just as she raised glowing eyes to Rob, her features radiating all the excitement of heady new love.

Lucille bustled across. Her mouth wore a smile, but her eyes were frosty and disapproving. 'Gaynor, honey,' she said in the voice of sweet reason. 'I think we should help instead of just wasting time with all this fooling. I'm sure there must be something useful we can do. Isn't that so, Hofi?'

Beth caught the inside of her lip to disguise her own smile as Hofi nodded seriously.

'Thank you, yes. Allan is testing the depth, but in any case it will be a good idea to take everything off the floor of the vehicles. There are some large plastic bags in the net pockets on the back of the seats. Please you put all coats, handbags, blankets, and any other thing into the bags, and then we tie them on the roof with other luggage.'

Lucille nodded, but as she turned to her daughter, Hofi went on, 'Gaynor, please you come with me. We must move all the vegetable racks off the floor of the trailer. I think is good idea also to check all cupboard bolts and catches. Sometimes in the rivers are many big stones and the trailer is going so . . .' She made lurching, tipping motions with her hands. Turning, she seemed surprised that Lucille was still there. 'There is a problem?' she enquired.

Lucille drew a breath, hesitated, shot a venomous look at Rob and another of ill-disguised frustration at her daughter, who gazed back blank-faced. Then she closed her mouth with a snap and shook her fluffy, lacquered head.

'So, I think we must hurry,' Hofi said gently.

Beth felt a pang of sympathy and automatically raised her camera to catch Lucille's retreat, shoulders slumped, as she vanished between the Land Rovers.

Lucille only wanted what was best for her daughter and, by her standards, Allan Bryce was a far better catch than Rob Wilson. It wasn't proving easy for her to accept that Gaynor had a right to make her own choices, especially when, in a mother's eyes, the choice was a poor one.

The various tasks took only minutes to complete, then they all returned to the river bank to watch Allan.

'Why is he so far upstream?' Eugene demanded. 'The river's twice as wide up there.'

'But is not so deep and not so fast,' Gunnar said without looking round.

Yet as Beth raised the camera, she could see the water eddying over Allan's knees. His foot slipped and the safety rope pulled taut as he stumbled on the edge of a stone. Her heart lurched.

'What's he doing?' Eugene muttered aloud. 'Why don't he go straight across? The way he's moving now, he's gonna reach the other side yards down from where he started.'

'There's quite a strong current,' Rob explained. 'It will almost certainly carry the vehicles downstream a bit. So it's better to set off upstream of the place you want to land, and cross on a diagonal. That way you're going with the current instead of fighting against it, and you should end up where you want to be.'

Eugene grunted and they both turned to watch Allan wading towards them, placing his feet carefully as the swift-flowing water foamed around his waders.

'With luck,' Rob added softly, and an icy shiver trickled down Beth's spine.

'Why are we crossing now?' she ventured. 'I thought Allan said it was better to cross in the morning when the flow was at its lowest.' Even using his name gave her a warm glow inside.

Gunnar glanced over his shoulder. 'With this river it make no difference. Sure it come from the glacier, but in July and August is much melt water, and level is high day and night. For Hofi we must cross now.' Gunnar bestowed a proud, loving glance on his wife. 'If we do not, we maybe not get to airstrip in time.' He went down to meet Allan who had just reached the bank.

'It's dicey,' Beth heard him say. 'There's a strong current and the bottom is treacherous, lots of loose boulders and sharp stones. Try and keep to that line.' She snapped him as he turned to indicate, with an outstretched arm, a suggested route through the grey, tumbling water. This one was not for Eugene, but for her own private collection. It captured the essence of the man she loved more completely than words ever could.

'OK.' Gunnar scratched his bearded chin, his eyes narrowing as he gauged distance and angle. 'So, I go first with trailer, yes?'

Allan gave a brief nod. 'Just as a precaution, Gunnar, loosen the fan belt. If you hit a deep spot, you'll have water spraying all over the engine and I can't see the repellent or a plastic bag being enough protection against that.'

A silent line, they watched Gunnar manoeuvre further up the river's edge to where it widened and the bank was slightly less steep. Then, facing slightly downstream, he eased down into the fast-flowing water and started across.

Both Land Rover and trailer swayed alarmingly, often in opposite directions, putting enormous strain on the coupling, as the wheels lurched over the rock-strewn river bed. The rushing water was so thick with silt Gunnar had no way of knowing what lay beneath the wheels.

After taking a photograph, Beth lowered the camera, gripping it tightly as she watched.

'This is worse than those disaster movies,' Gaynor whispered to Rob. 'The suspense is killing me. Why is he going so slowly?'

'To avoid building up a bow wave,' Rob replied, putting an arm around her shoulders. 'It could flood the engine. He mustn't stop either for the same reason. Only a few more yards now. He's almost there.'

As the words left his mouth the Land Rover seemed to stagger sideways, rearing up then jolting down and settling at an odd angle.

Automatically, Beth raised the camera, her finger on the

button. She heard the engine note rise and strain, saw the
vehicle shudder, but the expected jerk forward did not
come.

Gunnar rolled down his window.

'Are you stuck, or is it a flat?' Allan shouted.

'Near-side front tyre, I think,' Gunnar called back, gently
and continuously revving the engine to keep it ticking over.

'Rob,' Allan demanded crisply, 'have you brought some
spare boots?'

Rob grimaced and nodded, murmuring under his breath,
'Pneumonia, here I come.'

'Sorry, but you'll have to give me a hand to unhitch the
trailer. There's no way Gunnar will get out without cutting
the tyre to pieces or buckling the wheel if he tries towing
that extra weight.'

Beth bent and dipped her hand in the water. The intense
cold took her breath away. For an instant her fingers felt as
though they were burning, then the bitter cold numbed her
hand completely. Snatching it out, she stuck it under her
arm as she stood up, chewing her lip at the gnawing ache as
feeling gradually returned. Her fingers had been in the
water less than half a minute. Though the thick socks and
stout walking boots Rob and Gunnar had on would save
their feet from the stones, they were no protection against
the water which was almost thigh deep in places. Even
Allan's waders, while allowing him to stay dry, would not
keep out the cold.

In the river, the Land Rover's engine coughed and
spluttered as Gunnar nursed it, coaxing it to keep running

Without taking his eyes from the damaged vehicle, Allan
raised his voice. 'Beth?'

Startled, she hurried to him, aware of everyone's gaze.

'I want you to drive Gunnar's Land Rover up on to the
far bank.' He fixed her with a cool, dispassionate gaze
which, even though she could appreciate the necessity for

total commitment to the job in hand, aroused both anger and envy in her. Why couldn't she be like that? Why, when she looked at him, did she still taste his kiss and feel the warm, insistent pressure of his hands on her body? With enormous effort, she forced the thoughts aside the concentrated on what he was saying.

'We'll be wasting valuable time if I have to take mine in to tow his out and then go back for the trailer. Once his engine stops . . . ' He didn't bother to finish. Even with her limited knowledge of such things Beth realised that such damage would be impossible to repair out here. The loss of a vehicle would mean not only the abandonment of the whole trip, but severe difficulties in getting them all back to civilisation. 'Can you do it?'

As she nodded, gritting her teeth, Eugene demanded, 'Why don't I do that for you? I wanna help.'

Impatience, swiftly controlled, flitted across Allan's features. 'I don't suppose you've driven one of these before?'

'No,' Eugene admitted, 'but, hell, it can't be——'

'Beth has,' Allan broke in smoothly, 'and we're running out of time. In any case, Beth is lighter than you and I want as little weight as possible on that damaged wheel.' He turned away, closing the conversation.

'How the hell does he *know* she can drive the thing?' Eugene demanded of his wife, clearly disgruntled.

Lucille shrugged crossly. 'Why ask me? Seems there's a lot going on around here no one wants to tell us about.'

'Right, on to my back,' Allan ordered Beth, 'and keep your feet high.'

Swallowing hard, Beth stuck her arm through the camera strap.

'Hadn't you better leave that here?' Allan said. 'It looks expensive. I don't suppose a ducking would improve it.'

'No way,' Beth was adamant. She settled the camera more

comfortably just above her hip. 'This is the reason I'm
here, or had you forgotten.'

'I haven't forgotten anything,' he said, dangerously quiet.

'Anyway,' Beth felt her throat constrict, 'unless you
intend to drop me, it won't get wet.'

'Just remember your priority is——'

'I know exactly what I'm supposed to do.' Beth kept her
voice steady with an effort. 'Shall we go?'

Her arms clasped across the front of his shoulders, she
clung to him as he waded out into the river, placing his feet
carefully. The gusting wind added to their problems.

His arms were hooked firmly around her legs and her
cheek brushed his hair. She inhaled his warm, musky scent
and a tongue of sweet fire leapt within her at the play of his
back muscles against her breast and inner thighs.

'You hang on tight there, Beth,' Eugene shouted, 'else
both of you will end up in the water.'

'He really does have a genius for stating the obvious,'
Allan gritted under his breath and Beth giggled, forgetting
for one brief, heady moment her nervousness and the
responsibility that rested on her.

She held her breath as his foot slipped and he stumbled
slightly, deliberately relaxing her arms so that she would
not unbalance him.

'Are you all right?' Allan's voice was strangely rough.

'I'm fine,' Beth returned lightly. It was the truth. Despite
the precariousness of the situation, she hadn't the slightest
qualm that he might fall or drop her, though his feet must
be frozen by now.

'If there was anyone else——' he began, and she flinched
inwardly. So much for the imagined vote of confidence. He
hadn't asked her because he had faith in her, she was simply
the last resort. 'But there isn't,' she broke in. 'Don't worry,
Allan.' She tried, not altogether successfully, to keep
bitterness out of her voice. 'I'll do my best to get the Land

Rover those few yards to the bank without causing any further damage.'

She felt him tense. 'It wasn't the bloody Land Rover I was——' He bit the sentence off with such savagery she didn't dare ask him to finish what he had started to say.

The Land Rover had a left-hand drive, so Gunnar was on the downstream side. One small mercy, Beth thought.

Sheltered behind the barrier created by the vehicle, the water lapped level with the sill as Gunnar opened the door and stepped out into the river. His face contorted briefly when the icy water flooded into his boots. Swiftly, he guided Beth's feet as she slid from Allan's back.

She grabbed the steering-wheel and quickly sought the pedals. The engine coughed, then over-revved wildly as she tried, with legs that felt weak and trembly, to judge the right amount of pressure. She tensed, waiting for Allan to explode. Cold sweat dampened the back and underarms of her shirt as she cajoled the reluctant engine to keep going, and she guessed that Allan's continued silence must have cost him dear.

Carefully he closed the door. 'Stay in the lowest gear and just take it steady,' he ordered.

If the engine died now and the expedition had to be abandoned it would be entirely her fault.

'As soon as the trailer is unhooked I'll shout, then you get going. OK?'

She nodded, moistening lips that were paper-dry as she stared through the windscreen at the turbulent, grey water. It wasn't far, three yards at most. Once the front wheels were on the gently rising gravel bank . . .

'Beth,' Allan's voice, as he leaned forward to the open window, was gentle, 'you'll do fine, sweetheart, just relax.'

She jerked round, but he had gone. Suddenly she felt very much alone. Which was ridiculous, she told herself firmly. Allan, Rob and Gunnar were only a few feet away. Her foot moved on the accelerator and she gazed at the wing mirror, straining to see what was happening. *Sweetheart, he had called her sweetheart.*

Hofi was already in the driving-seat of Allan's vehicle, easing down the bank and into the water.

'OK, Beth, on your way.'

Though she was poised, waiting for the shout, it still made her jump. Her foot jerked, the engine roared, then spluttered, and Beth's knuckles turned white. 'Don't die on me, please don't die on me,' she prayed, and everything else was forgotten as she depressed the clutch, enagaged the lowest gear then, gripping the steering-wheel as if it were her lifeline, she gently pressed down the throttle and let the clutch in.

There was no time to wonder how Hofi was doing, or how long the three men could stand the bone-chilling cold.

The engine note rose. The vehicle juddered. Beth kept the pressure steady. 'Come on, *come on,*' she beseeched.

The Land Rover lifted a fraction. The back wheels slithered sideways on the loose stones and Beth tasted the salty tang of blood as her teeth pierced her lip.

With agonising slowness, the Land Rover limped forward. Inch by shuddering inch, it crept towards the bank, jolting over the rocky bottom with a lurching movement that jarred her teeth.

As though hypnotised, Beth stared at the gravel bank, willing it nearer. She reached it, letting her breath out in a shaky gust, and pressed on up to the level ground at the top.

Switching off the engine, she closed her eyes for an instant. Every muscle ached. She felt as though she'd run a marathon. *But she'd made it.*

A grin spread over her face. She jumped out, punching the air with a clenched fist, opening her mouth to give a triumphant yell, and closed it again, feeling rather foolish. No one was taking the slightest notice of her.

Hofi had managed to drive Allan's Land Rover into the river in front of the trailer. But it was too far upstream and the three men were working feverishly to haul the trailer round so that they could reach the coupling.

Beth could hear the explosive grunts of effort and watched the trailer rear up on one side as the wheel rode up on a hidden rock.

Conditioned reflex had the camera to her eye and her finger on the button, recording the drama as it unfolded.

Commands were shouted, the Land Rover edged forward and turned downstream. Heaving and straining, their faces contorted, the three men pulled. The trailer bumped and splashed forward.

At the same instant, Eugene, who had been shifting from one foot to the other in an agony of frustration at being relegated to the sidelines, plunged down the bank. 'Lemme give you some help!' he bawled.

'Neil!'

'Stay where you are!' Gunnar and Allan shouted in unison. Too late.

Eugene had taken several strides into the foaming water, when his face went white and he clutched at his chest. 'Jeez!' he gasped, and staggered, collapsing with a splash to his knees.

Lucille and Gaynor both screamed. With a final frantic heave the socket slipped over the ball-hitch and the coupling was secured. Gunnar dived into the driving-seat and Hofi scrambled over to the passenger side out of the way.

Rob and Allan splashed and stumbled towards Eugene, catching him as he was about to tumble forwards. They dragged him out on to the bank where he lay unmoving. Gaynor had her arm around her mother, trying to stop the shrill screams.

Gunnar drove up on to the level and Hofi leapt out. Lowering her camera, Beth ran forward to meet her.

'Quick, Beth, help me,' Hofi panted, reaching for the ball-hitch. 'We must——'

'No, Hofi, don't,' Beth warned. 'The strain——'

'But Eugene——'

'Eugene is OK, is shock only.' Gunnar came up behind his wife, his waterlogged boots squelching, and moved her aside with a firmness that clearly surprised her.

'How do you know? Are you sure?' Beth and Hofi demanded simultaneously.

'I am guessing,' he shrugged. 'But if I am wrong, will it help him if you lose our baby? Now, you fetch sleeping-bags and dry clothes for Eugene,' he directed his wife, 'then make hot drinks. Beth, you come.'

'Eugene is not the only one who needs dry clothes.' Beth darted an anxious glance across the river. Allan was crouched beside Eugene's motionless form. Lucille had stopped screaming and knelt at her husband's other side. Rob comforted Gaynor. *Oh, God, he couldn't be* . . . Even as the dreadful thought formed, Allan beckoned Lucille forward as Eugene turned his head, looking for her.

Relief left Beth weak. Eugene was alive and conscious.

Gunnar flashed her a knowing grin. 'You worry maybe Allan catch cold, eh?'

'Allan can take care of himself,' she retorted quickly, furious at the swift heat in her cheeks and at Gunnar's bland nod.

'Sure he can.' The big Icelander motioned her forward. 'And so can you. So why you are both not happy?'

She was spared the ordeal of trying to find an answer by his laconic instruction, 'OK, Beth. *Up.*'

Finding strength she had no idea she possessed, Beth helped him unhitch the trailer, supporting the towbar on a large flat stone.

As Hofi loosened the ropes securing the luggage, Gunnar jumped back into the Land Rover, spun it round and roared back down to the river.

CHAPTER EIGHT

HAD IT been a slip of the tongue revealing his true feelings? Or a deliberate ploy to boost her confidence and so achieve his aim of getting the damaged Land Rover saftely ashore? *Sweetheart.* It brought back so many memories.

Beth watched Allan and Rob pitch the last of the tents in the lee of a rock cliff. They were camped in a small oasis a short distance from the river. Facing west, the protected hollow was filled with golden light and long shadows. The late evening sun hung just above the horizon, a huge red ball, firing the towering masses of cloud with a spectacular blaze of orange, crimson and purple.

The short grass, though coarse and rough, was soothing to the eyes after so much bare rock and black gravel. Fed from a spring, sweet-tasting crystal-clear water fell ten feet from a lip of rock into a deep pool.

The two Land Rovers were parked at the entrance to the hollow with a line slung between them from which the wet clothes billowed in the breeze. They would soon be dry. The boots were another matter. With no trees or scrub to provide fuel for a fire, there was no means of drying them quickly. Rob had suggested the oven, but Hofi, mindful of her reputation as cook and the lingering after-effects of certain smells, vetoed the idea, pointing out that all the men except Eugene had a spare pair.

Beth surveyed the camp-site from her vantage point on a grassy knoll an equal distance from the tents on one side and the vehicles on the other.

Gunnar had changed the wheel and was repairing the damaged tyre, though it would be used only in the direst emergency.

Hofi and Gaynor had cleared away the remains of the meal and were in the trailer washing up.

Wrapped in a sleeping-bag for extra warmth, Eugene was propped up against a smooth, sloping rock. He had refused to remain in a tent or one of the Land Rovers, afraid he might miss something. Lucille sat beside him, sketching.

Behind Beth, the stream carrying water from the falls chuckled softly over its pebble bed as it flowed out of the oasis and away across the barren plateau. The sun warmed her face and cast mellow light on to the notebook resting on her knees. Her camera lay on the aluminium case by her feet. she was listing the contents of each numbered roll of film, trying hard to concentrate as she toyed with the possibility of writing a book about their journey.

The idea had grown as a result of Rob's suggestion while they ate, of captions for some of the photographs. The resulting hilarity when they all tried to outdo one another had dispelled the strain and exhaustion and drawn them together.

As Gunnar had correctly surmised, Eugene's attack had been simply a shock reaction to the icy water. But though everyone, including Eugene himself, was making light of it, Beth sensed the incident had taken more out of him than anyone realised, not only in physical terms, but in shattering his belief in himself and his ability to match the younger men.

During the meal he had laughed and joked with the rest of them. But now, as everyone went about their tasks and he no longer had to put up a good front, he looked suddenly old and frail.

For Beth, the concept of a book, illustrated *and written* by herself, was an exciting one, a new challenge in career terms. She wondered what Oliver's reaction would be. As her agent, he usually sent her photographs to editors who provided their own copywriters.

But she was oddly reluctant to part with any of the pictures she had taken on this expedition. Granted, she didn't *have* to, this wasn't a commission, she was working in her own time and Eugene had the only claim to copies of the prints. Yet in the past she had frequently sold photographs taken in her off-duty moments. In fact she could remember two, both prize-winners, which had reimbursed her the cost of the trip.

But this time was different. No one, without having been here, could possibly do justice to this unique, spell-binding land, a land still being formed. A land of ice-fields and steam vents, of black, barren deserts and boiling geysers, of vast, treacherous glaciers and volcanoes spewing out red-hot rivers of molten rock.

Beth was surprised at the strength of her possessive feeling for the photographs. Then, with a flash of insight, she understood. *Allan.*

How like this land he was, a man of frost and fire, so cold and forbidding on the surface, yet volatile and passionate underneath.

He permitted few people beyond the barrier he had erected in childhood, protection against a stiff, hard-driving father who, like many military men, had been unable to show his very real affection for his son, equating any display of emotion with weakness.

The marriage had broken up when he was eleven and, at his father's insistence and expense, he had been sent to boarding-school, 'to make a man of him'.

His mother had been reluctant, but wanted the best for him, and had her hands full with his two younger sisters.

With a vividness and poignancy that brought sudden tears welling up, Beth recalled the first time Allan had told her he loved her. The moment had been for him a combination of agonising admission and triumphant escape from the shackles of the past.

It was the first time he had spoken those words despite a past which, while in no way lurid, made it perfectly clear he was a normal man with healthy appetites. Having learned, during quiet conversations late into the night, something of his background and childhood, she knew what a giant step the commitment represented for him. *And for her.* For, once Allan had openly acknowledged that he loved her, their marriage had been a foregone conclusion. A few weeks later they had made their vows and Beth had discovered a happiness beyond her wildest dreams. Then, a spectre from the past, Shalana, had appeared, and her whole world had crumbled.

Yet, even then, before she knew the truth, almost smothered beneath anger, bitterness and grief, a tiny spark had remained stubbornly alive. She had refused, then, to acknowledge its existence. Now she had no choice.

That was why the photographs were so important, why she could not allow anyone else to write the commentary. The truth had to be faced. This expedition was a turning-point in her life.

Once again fate had brought Allan and her together. For her the spark still burned, a fact that aroused more apprehension than joy. Ties she had believed severed beyond repair were once more drawing them together. More than that, *they were still married.*

Gunnar's laconic observation that neither she *nor Allan* was happy had jolted her. Was there a chance that some of the old feeling remained in him too?

Until the sandstorm all his contact with her seemed to have been fired by anger. Even if the others had not recognised it, she certainly had.

But that last kiss had been so different. Tender, intimate, it had been a vivid reminder of past joys and a promise of more to come. A wave of hungry yearning swept her, catching her breath in her throat. As she had driven the damaged Land Rover out of the river, *he had called her sweetheart.*

'Right, everyone, may I have your attention.' Allan left the tents and moved towards Eugene. Rob followed close behind, his eyes lighting up as Gaynor emerged from the trailer in front of Hofi.

Immersed in her own thoughts, Beth had not noticed Allan approaching, and she jumped, dropping her pen. It clattered on to the aluminium case and he glanced round.

Her cheeks aflame, Beth bent quickly to retrieve it. Until she knew for certain where she stood, what *he* felt, she dared not reveal any more of her growing confusion, *or hope.*

That he felt *something* was clear from the lines of strain at the corners of his eyes and mouth. Her heart swelled as if to choke her.

Within moments they were all sitting or sprawled on the grass facing Allan. With the acute perception that was so much a part of her talent, Beth noticed the subtle changes that had taken place in all of them. It was more than just a slight scruffiness of appearance. There was a new awareness of their dependence on one another, of the true meaning of team effort. Today they all sat closer to one another than they would have done a week ago.

She knew she too had changed since they had left Akureyri. Already it seemed they had been travelling a lot longer than a few days. In terms of self-discovery they were all, in their own ways, making a journey from which they would return different people.

She emerged from her reverie to hear Allan outlining the route for the following day.

'It will be pretty uncomfortable, I'm afraid. We have another lava field ahead of us, and two more rivers to cross.' A groan went up. 'However,' Allan raised his voice and calmly carried on, 'Gunnar assures me we shall not be faced with a repeat of today's problems.' Audible mutterings of relief greeted his words. 'Speaking of which, I would like to say how marvellously you all responded. Hofi and Gunnar reacted like the professionals they are. Considering their impending parenthood, Hofi could have been forgiven for being reluctant to take risks. In the event, she had to be forcibly prevented from trying to unhitch the trailer all by herself!'

Hofi blushed and flashed her husband a radiant smile.

Allan turned his piercing gaze on Beth, his expression sombre, and she swallowed nervously.

'It must have felt pretty damn lonely sitting in the middle of the river waiting for us to uncouple the trailer, knowing that if the engine stopped it would be virtually impossible to start again, which would have meant curtains for the expedition.'

Beth's eyes widened. He had captured her thoughts exactly.

'It's the sort of situation that calls for a great deal of courage.'

All round there were murmurs of agreement, but Beth scarcely heard them, tensing as Allan's eyes grew cold. 'Fortunately, on this occasion, Beth showed she had what it took. It is thanks to her we are able to go on.'

Rob whistled and led the applause. Though she smiled, dipping her head in shy gratitude at the grinning faces and clapping hands, inside Beth was tormented. Only she recognised the significance of his phrase *on this occasion*.

She had to talk to him, as soon as possible. She had to explain why she had acted the way she had. But would he listen? Or were his hurt and anger too deep? *She had to try.*

Vaguely Beth realised Allan had finished speaking and they were all chatting quietly among themselves. She felt her arm nudged and looked down to see Rob who jerked his head towards Lucille.

'That woman,' he muttered furiously. 'She just won't give up.'

Beth turned to see what he was talking about. Lucille was gazing up at Allan, simpering and kittenish.

'. . . such a lovely girl, a real credit to her daddy and me.'

'She is indeed,' Allan agreed and, with a polite half-smile, started to move away. But Lucille fastened both hands round his arm in the manner of an old-fashioned southern belle, and hung on, effectively halting him.

'I guess you're a mite surprised what a help she's been on this expedition.' Lucille batted her eyelashes at him.

Rob and Beth exchanged a bemused glance. 'Gaynor?' Beth whispered.

Rob nodded. 'Lucille Brennan is a perfect example of the American matriarch.'

'And you still want her daughter?' Beth's tone was dry.

'The sooner the better,' Rob grinned, 'before the programming takes effect.'

'Not at all,' Allan was saying, 'I made it clear before we set off that everyone had to contribute.'

'So you did,' Lucille nodded vigorously. 'I guess an eminent man like yourself must do a lot of entertaining when you're at home.'

Even Allan looked momentarily taken aback at this unexpected change of direction.

'Well, I——'

'My Gaynor is just the best little hostess in Dallas. You would not believe some of the names that have sat around her table, businessmen, politicians, filmstars. And of course there's her charity work too. She has personally raised thousands of dollars for the League——'

'Momma,' Gaynor broke in in quiet desperation, her complexion bright pink, 'I don't think Dr Bryce wants to hear all that.'

'Aw honey, don't be shy,' Lucille twinkled and Rob looked as though he was about to be sick. 'It's no use being so gifted and beautiful if no one appreciates it. You got every right to be proud of your achievements. As for Allan here not wanting to know, why that's nonsense. Travelling the world like he does, he meets all kindsa folk.' She turned to Allan once more, dimpling up at him. 'Isn't that so?'

Allan nodded briefly, but before he could utter a word, Lucille was once again in full flow.

'But a man needs a comfortable home to come back to, and a loving wife to welcome him.'

Allan's eyes met Beth's and her heart contracted. The contact was fleeting, but the after-shock lingered, tingling along every nerve.

The others had given up all pretence at continuing their own conversations, openly watching and listening.

'Now I know it's not easy these days to find the right kinda woman.' Lucille was as relentless as a juggernaut. 'All this here Women's Liberation has filled girls' heads with a lot of nonsense about equality and careers.' Rob and Beth exchanged another glance. 'There's far too many of them trying to *be* men. Now where's the sense in that? They're losing their special feminine qualities and that's a real shame. Don't you think so, Allan?' She didn't wait for him to reply.

'Some may call me old-fashioned, but I believe a woman is happiest with a home to run, a man to care for and babies to rear. That's how Eugene and me raised our little girl. Sure, she's made a coupla mistakes, but that could happen to anybody, and she'll make a fine wife for a man worthy of all her special talents.'

'*Momma,*' Gaynor gasped in an agony of embarrassment.

'You listen to your mother,' Eugene growled. 'She talks a whole lotta sense. A man don't want a competitor when he comes home nights, he wants a woman who knows her place.'

Hofi and Gunnar looked at each other in bewilderment. Beth could hear Rob grinding his teeth.

'We've all grown very fond of Gaynor in the short time

we've known her.' Allan's deep voice was resonant with controlled anger. Beth knew it was only the hope of sparing Gaynor further embarrassment that prevented him telling Lucille exactly what he thought of her blatant attempt at matchmaking.

Oblivious of the undercurrents, Lucille preened.

'Her sense of humour, her willingness to help and her lack of complaint have endeared her to all of us.'

There was a general murmur of agreement and Gaynor flushed again, her eyes suspiciously bright as they sought Rob's. She smiled tremulously.

Allan looked down at Lucille. 'As well as being very beautiful, your daughter is a nice person. I'd consider it an honour to marry her.'

In the sudden hush, Gaynor gaped at him, speechless. Rob and Beth glanced at one another, both openly shocked, though for entirely different reasons, while Lucille's plump bosom swelled with pride and she smirked her triumph and satisfaction.

'*However.*' As the single word dropped like a pebble into a glassy pool and the ripples spread wider and wider, Allan prised Lucille's hands from his arm. Beth stopped breathing altogether. 'Gaynor has already made her choice. I hope she doesn't consider me impertinent if I say it's a wise one. She and Rob will make each other very happy.'

Beth stared at the ground, her heartbeat loud and rapid in her ears as she let out a shaky breath.

Lucille's face was ugly with shock and disappointment. 'But I meant . . . I thought *you*——' she blurted before she could stop herself.

Gaynor closed her eyes, balling her small hands into fists. 'Momma,' she groaned.

Rob leapt up and went to her side, enfolding her in gentle arms. She buried her face in his shoulder.

'Me?' Allan sounded surprised. 'I never stood a chance,'

he smiled. Rob and Gaynor both shot him glances of gratitude and appreciation. 'Besides,' he turned his head so that his gaze fell on Beth, his eyes slate-hard, derisive, 'I am already married.'

Hofi and Gunnar talked softly in their own language, their eyes darting from Allan to Beth, who had not had time or opportunity to tell Hofi the truth about Shalana. She started to smile at Hofi, wanting her friend to understand that all was well. But Allan had not finished. Still looking at Beth, he added quietly, 'A situation I intend to remedy.' Scooping up his parka from the ground by his feet, he slung it around his shoulders.

All Beth could hear was the sound of the waterfall. It grew louder and louder until the rushing water seemed to fill her head. She felt dizzy and very cold, and sucked breath into lungs that hurt. *No, He couldn't meant it. Not now. They had only just——She had to talk to him.*

'You want I come help you look for the coupling-lock?' Gunnar called as Allan started towards the barren plateau.

Allan shook his head. 'I won't go back more than a mile or so. Get some rest, and make sure Hofi does too.'

Gunnar roared with laugher. 'Now you are asking impossible things, but I try.'

Already Allan was several yards away, his long easy stride swiftly widening the distance between himself and the camp.

Reaching blindly, automatically for her camera, Beth stood up. 'I—I'm just . . . ' She gestured towards the vast emptiness beyond the camp-site, her fixed smile making her cheeks tremble.

'Don't worry about the camera case, Beth,' Gaynor called after her. 'I expect you want to catch the light. I'll take it to the tent when I go.'

Beth waved and walked on, not daring to look back, unable to keep the fear from her face.

'Well, she's certainly not wasting any time,' Lucille muttered just loudly enough for Beth to hear. 'Not that she'd have stood a chance if our Gaynor had been interested in him.'

Beth checked momentarily. *You stupid woman,* she screamed silently, *you don't understand anything.* But her rage, born of terror and frustration, drained away almost immediately. She wasn't being fair. Of course Lucille didn't understand. How could she? She had no way of knowing that the marriage Allan spoke of, *and the intended remedy,* involved Beth.

Eugene followed his wife towards their tent, trailing his sleeping-bag behind him.

Beth started running, stumbling over the rock-strewn ground. Already Allan seemed so far away.

Thoughts, incidents, snatches of memory, buzzed in her head like a swarm of angry bees.

He had called her sweetheart. In the Land Rover he had kissed her so tenderly, as though she were precious to him. The tenderness had blossomed into a remembered passion that had left them both shaken and breathless. It had not been one-sided, he had been stirred as deeply as she.

She recalled his reaction to the news of Hofi's baby. She could still hear the harshness, and the undertone of agony as he gripped her upper arm. *This is Gunnar's baby too. Do you think that I . . . if we had . . .?*

'Allan!' she cried, her voice hoarse and cracked with strain.

He stopped. It was almost as if he had expected, been waiting for her shout. Lowering his head, keeping his back to her, he stood immobile as she caught up with him.

'Please,' Beth panted, white-faced and chilled despite the headlong dash, 'please wait. There is something I must tell you.'

He turned his head to look at her. His face was an expressionless mask. Only his eyes seemed alive, blazing with a torment that made Beth flinch. Then the shutters slammed down and they became opaque and somewhere in the darkest corner of her mind Beth heard an echo, *too late, too late*.

Allan looked away, staring straight ahead. 'I want a divorce.'

Beth recoiled, feeling the last vestige of colour drain from her face. Even though from what he had said back at camp she expected it, the actual words still stunned her.

'It will be quite straightforward,' he went on tonelessly. 'We have been separated for two years. I believe the current phrase is *irretrievable breakdown.*'

'No, Allan. Please.' She was so cold her mouth felt rubbery, as though she had no control over her facial muscles. 'Fate, coincidence, call it what you like, has brought us together again. Couldn't we at least give it another chance?' She could hear the desperation in her voice, the pleading, but was past caring. Pride was irrelevant. She was fighting for a future.

The expression in his eyes turned her blood to ice. 'Another chance?' His smile was as bleak as an arctic winter. 'I gave you everything I had. *I loved* you. But it wasn't enough. At the first sign of a problem you ran.' His contempt seared like a flame. 'Do you take me for a fool?' His face was dark with anger and rekindled suffering. 'You hurt me far more than I could ever hurt you, Beth. But never again. No woman, least of all you, will ever have that power again.'

His admission elated and terrified her.

'I was wrong,' she cried. 'I should have waited and talked it out with you. But I was afraid. You see, Father——' His profile was hard, unyielding. She swallowed, forcing herself to go on. Surely he'd understand? 'My father had several—*affaires*. My mother adored him and when she found out, as she always did, he promised it would never happen again. Because my mother loved him and wanted to keep the family together, she believed him. Only it *did* happen again and again. I grew up with that, all the misery and suspicion, the uncertainty and atmospheres, and I swore I would never, *ever* allow it to happen to me.' Beth's mouth was dry and her throat ached. 'So when Shalana came—I thought—I didn't stop to *reason;* I was a child again, and I ran.

She waited, nerves tightened to breaking-point, for his reaction.

For a fleeting instant the mask cracked. 'You never told me,' he said softly. 'You never told me,' he repeated. But this time it was an accusation. Voice and expression hardened. 'It makes no difference. *I* was not your father.'

Beth's precarious control snapped and she exploded. 'You hypocrite! You can make the rules but you don't have to obey them, is that what you're saying? If *you* had bothered to tell *me* about Shalana, *none of this need be happening.'*

She was rigid with tension, breathing quickly, her heart pounding.

The silence went on and on. But just as she was beginning to hope, 'It's too late,' he said flatly. 'You might as well accept it.'

For a moment she was tempted. Pride, self-respect and logic all urged her to admit defeat. She had suffered too, and to go on trying, inviting more pain, in the face of such implacable hostility, defied reason. But, like a thorn under her skin, a tiny voice inside her insisted that something about his demand for a divorce didn't add up.

'No.' She shook her head with a calmness that amazed her. 'I won't accept it.'

A muscle flickered beside his mouth and she knew she had startled him. Guided only by intuition, she pressed on. 'I hurt you dreadfully and I'll carry that guilt to my grave.' Her nails bit into her palms. 'But seeing you again, being

with you, *learning the truth*, has made me realise how much
. . . how much I still love you.' The muscle jumped again
and her eyes were drawn to it, held by it. 'And no matter
how often or how strongly you deny it, I know that
somewhere, deep down, under all your anger and
unhappiness, you still love me.'

'Because I kissed you?' he shot back. 'Aren't you being a
little naïve?'

Her face aflame, Beth kept her head high. 'No,' she
announced quietly. 'You can have your divorce, Allan, if
that's what you really want.'

He couldn't resist a sideways glance that betrayed
surprise, and something else. *Doubt? Unease?*

'It's only a piece of paper.'

'Just like the marriage certificate,' he retorted savagely.

'Don't you see?' Her voice was growing hoarse from the
effort of trying to make him understand. 'It's not the piece
of paper that matters. You and Shalana had a marriage
certificate, but you didn't have a marriage. We *did*, you and
I. It was solid and real. Yes, it was brief, and I nearly
wrecked it through my fear and lack of trust.'

'Nearly?' He was bitterly scornful.

She nodded. 'It wasn't a total write-off, Allan. You could
have sued for divorce any time in the last two years, citing
desertion, but you didn't.'

He looked away, his expression stony. But he did not
argue.

'God knows I've paid,' Beth said quietly, 'and I'll go on
paying the rest of my life in regret for all the wasted time.
Nothing can wipe out the past. But it *is* the past. It doesn't
have to be the future too.'

Allan did not reply. Beth dared not say more. She had to
give him time. He was bitter and angry and, she conceded,
he had every right to be. *How he must have suffered.* She had
suffered too, and the fact that it had been her fault made it

doubly hard to hear.

They had both held back something of themselves and their past. Not through shame or deliberate deception. Both had simply believed the past irrelevant to their special relationship.

But it had, in fact, been a time-bomb. And a twist of fate, in the form of a dishonest solicitor, had lit the fuse and ignited an inevitable sequence of destruction.

'Goodnight, Allan,' Beth whispered and turned back towards the camp-site, suddenly more tired than she had ever been before in her life.

He did not reply. But his face, as he watched her walk away, was tormented. Beads of sweat gathered on his upper lip and he wiped them away with a savage gesture. How many kinds of fool was he? Why couldn't he wipe her out of his mind? Out of his life? This past year he had hardly thought of her at all. Except at odd moments when his guard was down. When a snatch of music, a certain perfume, a particular note of laughter had brought her back with such vividness the pain was paralysing.

But he had learned to deal with it. With cold, clear-eyed determination, he had conditioned himself to hate her. Hatred anaesthetised him, gave him an outlet in anger for a grief which could not have been deeper had she died.

The ploy had been successful until he had walked into Hofi's kitchen and seen her standing at the sink. The shock had been devastating.

Since then, driven by something outside his control, despising himself for his weakness, he had done more, much more than just look. He had touched her, held her close, tasted the compelling excitement of her body against his, and the sweet warmth of her mouth.

And even as, like a man drowning, he clung to the lifebelt of his hatred, he ached with need for the slender body in which, for such a short time, he had lost himself and found a peace he had never known before or since.

But she had run away. All right, so she hadn't known about Shani, and it must have been a terrible shock. And that business over her father would have left deep scars. But she didn't wait to ask, to find out the truth, she just left. What sort of love was that? And if they did somehow patch it up? What if one day they had a row? Would she walk out on him again? He would never be sure. Love? To hell with it. He could not go through that again.

His mouth thinned and his eyes became slivers of ice. He was in control once more. The decision was made.

CHAPTER NINE

HUDDLED in her sleeping-bag, a thick jumper over her pyjamas, woolly socks on her feet, mentally shattered, Beth slept. Twice during the night she came round to feel hot tears trickling down her face and a damp patch on the pillow beneath her cheek. But before she could escape, she was sucked down once more into vivid dreams filled with Allan.

For so long she had blocked him out of her thoughts. But the images, the memories, had been stored in her mind and now, like a tidal wave, they overwhelmed her. Touch and laughter, confidences exchanged, barriers pushed back, work discussed, and the long glorious hours of loving. Each night they had shut out the rest of the world and immersed themselves with delight in each other. She had never known such happiness. Yet sometimes in the dark hours, lying with Allan, their bodies still entwined, warm and drugged from lovemaking, a premonition, as light and cold as a snowflake, had brushed the peaceful surface of her mind, leaving a ripple of fear. Could it really last?

When she awoke, brought to the surface by Gaynor's gentle shake, she was emotionally numb. It was a relief to feel *nothing*. All the upheaval within her had gone, leaving her oddly calm.

'Time to move.' Gaynor looked at her more closely, concern knitting her brows. 'You OK?'

Beth nodded, a little too quickly. 'It's all this fresh air and exercise,' she murmured. Her eyes felt swollen and gritty. Her return to camp the previous night had gone unremarked. Everyone had been in their tents except Gaynor, who, to Beth's intense relief, had been with Rob. Beth had been able

157

to get ready for bed alone and was settled in her sleeping-bag, eyes closed, when Gaynor eventually came in.

Gaynor grimaced. 'If a herd of elephants had stampeded through the tent, I wouldn't have stirred.'

The tension that had begun to knot Beth's muscles ebbed away. No one had heard her weeping. 'Whose turn to get the water?' She smothered a yawn.

Gaynor groaned. 'Mine, 'I guess.' Fully dressed, she crawled towards the entrance and began to unzip the flaps. 'Gee, it sure feels chilly this morn—— *Well, would you look at that!*'

'What?' Beth struggled out of her sleeping-bag.

'Snow!' Gaynor squeaked, turning an incredulous face to Beth. 'Snow in *July!*'

'That's Iceland for you,' Beth mumurmed, 'unpredictable.' She turned quickly away at the sudden, knifing pain.

Shivering, she tugged off the thick jumper and pyjama top and began to dress, only one thought in her mind. *What would his answer be?*

'What wouldn't I give for a long soak in a hot bath,' Gaynor groaned. 'And a massage, and shampoo with buckets of conditioner.' She scrunched her hair in two handfuls, despair clouding her lovely face. 'What must I look like?' she wailed. 'It feels just awful.'

'Give it a good brushing and put it up,' Beth advised. 'Honestly, it looks super like that. It really suits you.'

'It does?' Gaynor sounded both dubious and surprised.

'Mmmm,' Beth nodded. 'It shows off your long neck and the shape of your face.' She struggled into her trousers, bent double in the confined space. 'You've got marvellous bone structure. Why hide it?'

Gaynor lowered her arms, letting her hair fall loose. 'You know, you're one of the kindest people I ever met.' She rummaged among the debris scattered all over her sleeping-bag and eventually found the brush.

You're wrong, you're wrong, Beth wanted to scream. Where had her kindness been when Shalana had needed it? *And Allan.*

Like morning mist, the numbness which had been cushioning her was dissolving. She felt lost. What would happen now? Would Allan give her the chance she had begged for? Or would he . . . She shied away from an alternative too dreadful to contemplate.

'Beth,' Gaynor began awkwardly. 'About last night.'

Beth froze for an instant, then sat down on her rumpled sleeping-bag to lace up her boots. 'Mmmm?'

'You didn't know, did you?' Gaynor twisted the brush round and round. 'About Allan being married, I mean.'

Beth lifted one shoulder, her fingers all thumbs as she fumbled with the laces. 'It did come as a bit of a shock,' she admitted truthfully. Gaynor didn't know they were talking at cross-purposes, and Beth was not going to enlighten her.

'Still,' Gaynor perked up, 'it sounds like he's planning to be a free man again soon.'

Beth's head jerked up, but she looked down again quickly as the blood drained from her face. She could not speak. Fortunately Gaynor seemed more concerned with making her point than in Beth's reaction.

'Now, don't get mad at me,' she appealed, 'I know you said you weren't interested in him an' all, but when he told Momma he was married and that he intended to do something about it, your face . . .' She broke off with a helpless gesture. 'Look, all I'm saying is you could be in with a chance.'

Beth could feel hysteria building up inside her. She didn't know whether to laugh or cry. Both were perilously near the surface.

'Allan Bryce has been taking a whole lotta interest in you,' Gaynor went on, determined to have her say, despite her companion's apparent lack of response. 'Only he's tried not to show it, if you know what I mean.'

Beth kept her head bent as she folded her pyjamas. *What*

was Gaynor saying? 'He——' she cleared her throat, 'he had to keep an eye on everyone. That's part of an expedition leader's job..

'I know *that.*' Gaynor was mildly impatient. She raked the brush through her hair twice more then paused, her voice soft and dreamy, a faraway expression on her face. 'But it's more. He watches you. I mean, he gets on with whatever he's doing, but his eyes follow *you.* I guess he think's no one's noticed. I wouldn't have except . . . well . . . for a while back there I was thinking maybe . . .' She shrugged, dismissing the idea. 'Anyway, that's history. You were right about Rob. He's really special. He's gentle and kind, but he's no pushover.' Her eyes shone and her mouth curved in a secret smile. With a visible effort she dragged herself back to the matter in hand. 'But when anyone asked where you were, or what you were doing, Allan knew,' she snapped her fingers, 'just like that.'

'What an imagination!' Beth teased. But her heart was racing and her hands, as she continued to pack, were unsteady.

'You can laugh,' Gaynor warned. 'But for a man who says he's already married, Allan Bryce sure has been showing an awful lot of interest in you.'

Beth remained silent. Gaynor didn't know how accurate her observations were. What would she have thought if she had seen them kissing? Would she have realised that their embraces were not the tentative exploration of sudden awareness, but the passionate fusion of lovers who knew other intimately?

She felt a sudden, overwhelming urge to confide the truth, that *she* was Allan's wife and it was *she* he was planning to leave.

Beth bit hard on her tongue. She could not do that. Though she longed for comfort and reassurance, it was a private matter between Allan and herself. To bring anyone else in would be an even greater betrayal of his trust. There was only Hofi, Hofi, who was friend to them both, who knew of their marriage. She *had* to talk to Hofi.

'Shall I give you a hand with the packing?' Gaynor pushed the last of the pins into the knot high on the back of the head.

Beth shook her head. 'I think it will be better if you help Hofi with breakfast. I can see to this lot. It's easier with only one of us in the tent.'

Gaynor sighed. 'How does it get so untidy?'

Beth grinned at her. 'Go on, and don't forget your jacket.' She thrust the velvet-soft leather into the girl's hands.

As soon as Gaynor had gone, Beth raced through the rest of the packing. Then pulling on a woolly hat and gloves, she zipped up her anorak, grabbed her camera, and crawled out of the tent.

Her breath condensed in a steaming cloud as she gazed at the snow blanketing the hollow. The pristine carpet was broken by Gaynor's footsteps leading towards the trailer where they were lost among all the others.

Beth started taking pictures. The snow crunched beneath her boots as she went to the entrance of their camp-site and looked out across the plateau.

The wind had dropped and in the silence the sounds from the camp seemed loud. She heard Hofi and Gaynor laughing above the clatter of pans. Eugene coughed, a hacking, painful sound. Rob was singing 'Oh, what a beautiful morning' as he filled the huge kettle in the stream. The scent of hot coffee drifted towards Beth and her mouth watered.

There was not a cloud in the sky. Pale pink on the eastern horizon, it ranged through coral, gold and primrose to aquamarine, turquoise and clear, translucent blue.

The snow sparkled, a white carpet sprinkled with diamond-dust, covering the black boulders and gravel, softening jagged outlines.

Hofi banged a saucepan with a metal spoon to call everyone to breakfast.

Beth looked for Allan, drinking in his tall figure, her heart pounding. She watched him talking briefly to Rob and at greater length to Gunnar. He smiled and winked at Gaynor as she emerged pink and laughing from the trailer to fetch more water. He bent to exchange a few words with Eugene who was sitting sideways on the front seat of the nearest Land Rover, the door open, and nodded to Lucille who, this morning, was devoting all her attention to her husband.

But not once did he glance at Beth. She knew he was aware of her. He had to be, or he would not be going to such lengths to ignore her.

As they both moved about the camp-site, their paths crossing and re-crossing, yet never quite close enough to necessitate speech, it was as though an invisible cord joined them, vibrating with a tension of which only they were aware.

He had warned her that first evening. She had sensed then that he would make her pay for staying with the expedition and reopening old wounds.

He had known he was still her husband even though she had not, and he had wanted her. But what now? Had reliving the past, the anguish he had suffered because of her, and the distintegration of all he believed in, purged him of all feeling for her but contempt? *No!*

The silent scream of denial came from a need beyond reason and logic. She had no more excuses. No more pretence that she didn't need him, that she was better off alone, and that loving someone cost too dear.

The price *was* high. But without love, *his* love, her life was empty, meaningless. Without Allan life became mere existence. Materially, she was indpendenet. Professionally, her star was rising. But emotionally she was as arid as a desert.

She did not want to lose him. With awful clarity she recalled the bitter set of his mouth and eyes that had pierced her like twin blades.

A shudder of fear shook her. Last evening he had commended her bravery in the river. That little incident paled to insignificance beside the courage she would need in the next few days.

Eugene was making a valiant effort to be bright and cheerful, but he refused any food and Lucille had to press him to drink his coffee.

Concerned, Beth studied him, fingering her camera. His cheeks had a hectic flush and his eyes an unnatural glitter. He coughed frequently, a hard painful sound, but he made light of it.

She took a candid shot, and saw Allan open the first-aid kit and remove some foil-packed tablets. It looked very much as though Eugene's plunge in the river had resulted in a chill.

No one lingered over breakfast. Without making a fuss, Allan was forcing the pace. They had to reach the airstrip by early afternoon and there was no way of knowing what conditions lay ahead of them.

As soon as the Land Rovers were loaded, the party were once more on their way.

Sitting silently beside Allan, as Rob and Gaynor chatted and laughed in the back, Beth pulled off her hat and gloves, unzipping her anorak as the heater warmed the air. She ran her fingers through her cropped curls. Her scalp itched and once more she thought longingly of a luxurious bath filled with steaming, scented water.

She gazed out through the windscreen. Already the snow was beginning to melt, dissolving as she watched. Tiny streams coursed through the gravel and over the smooth rock to join the river.

As they left the plateau, a cluster of bare hills rose steeply above the gently sloping lava.

The river flowed wide and shallow on their left, curving and bending as it sought the easiest route.

Then, as they approached another lava field, the going became much more difficult. The Land Rover slowed almost to a crawl as they lurched and jolted over the twisted, broken rock.

Beth clung to her seat, starting slightly as Gaynor leaned forward. Her rosy glow had faded to a sickly pallor. 'Sorry, you guys, but I can't take this. Can I get out and walk? I promise I won't lag behind. I mean, it's not as if you can get up much speed on a surface like this. Only——' The Land Rover gave a violent lurch and Gaynor groaned, closed her eyes, and swallowed audibly.

Allan braked. His arms were stretched out in front of him, his hands resting loosely on the top of the steering-wheel. Up ahead Gunnar had stopped as well and, as they watched, Hofi dived out, hand clamped over her mouth, and stumbled behind a large boulder.

For the first time that morning Allan looked directly at Beth, concern drawing his dark brows together. 'Hofi——' he began.

Beth felt a pang. 'I'll take care of her,' she said quickly. 'It will probably be better if we walk too, at least until we're through this.'

He gave a brief nod. Gaynor and Rob clambered out, Gaynor sighing with relief and Rob gently making fun of her even as he fastened her jacket and dropped a kiss on her forehead.

Allan revved the engine and was pulling away almost before Beth had closed the door.

She watched the vehicle crawl over the lumpy fissured rock. Surely he would talk to her soon? He couldn't intend to leave when they reached the glacier, without another word or backward glance. *Could he?*

Panic fluttered like a flock of dark wings and for a moment Beth couldn't breathe.

She forced herself to relax. There were still two days to go. He was probably waiting for a more suitable time. Possibly this evening, after they had seen Hofi safely on board the plane back to Akureyri. Then he would tell her. Then she would know.

Colour gradually returned to Hofi's cheeks as she and Beth followed Rob and Gaynor along the barely marked track.

Beth's camera was slung around her neck, but for once she had forgotten it and, in a soft, hesitant voice, she told Hofi the full story just as Allan had related it to her.

Her arm linked through Beth's, Hofi listened intently, her reactions reflected in her changing expression.

When Beth finished, elation coupled with hope lit Hofi's gentle eyes and lifted the corners of her mouth.

'So, you and Allan are still married to each other? But that is wonderful!'

Beth glanced at her friend, then looked ahead to the second Land Rover as it bumped and jolted across the uneven surface, and tried, unsuccessfully, to stifle a deepening apprehension.

'Hofi, I'm afraid—I think it's too late.'

Hofi stopped and, with a firm hand, pulled Beth round to face her. 'Is never too late,' she said with quiet intensity. 'Ten years I wait for our baby. I hope, I pray, I *believe* one day it will happen. Yes, sometimes the doubt come, and but I chase it away. No room for that.' She took Beth's hands. 'Gunnar say it no matter, we have each other and we are so lucky. He is right, but still, in my heart, I hope. Many times we are disappointed, but the love grow stronger. And with love, anything possible.'

She laid Beth's hand on her still flat abdomen. 'In there our baby is growing. You understand what I am saying?'

Beth nodded.

'You still love him.' Hofi made the words a statement.

Beth nodded again. 'I never stopped. God knows I tried——' Her voice wobbled and she cleared her throat.

'Then *fight,*' Hofi commanded. 'With enough love you will win.'

Beth bit her lip. If only it were that simple. Not only did she have to fight her own fear of rejection, she had to overcome his doubt.

Yet what was the alternative? To lose him by default? To give up and slink away? If she did that she did not deserve to win. Did she want to spend the rest of her life grieving over what might have been?

There were two points in her favour. In this ocean of doubts they were her life-raft. Allan and she were still legally man and wife. In the two years they had been apart, despite his bitter anger, he had done nothing about severing the legal bond that still united them. Surely that must mean something?

And there was no denying the attraction that existed between them. *It was even more potent than she remembered.*

Beth's spirits began to rise. She tucked her arm through Hofi's. 'I'll fight,' she vowed softly. 'I'll give it everything I've got.' A spasm tightened her features. 'But——' Before she could go further Hofi's hand covered her mouth, cutting her short.

'*No.* No buts.' Hofi shook her head decisively. 'No doubts. Think only of Allan and how it was between you before . . . '

Beth nodded, squeezing her arm, and drew in a deep, shaky breath.

They followed the track without further incident and, after crossing two more rivers, arrived at the landing-strip. A galvanised iron hut painted bright red offered shelter. The airstrip itself was simply a long, reasonably flat piece of bare ground marked on either side by big stones.

As everyone clambered out of the Land Rovers, the trouble started.

Gunnar came across to Allan, shaking his head. 'Eugene not fit to go on. He must leave with Hofi on the plane.'

Eugene staggered after him. 'I'm all right, I tell ya.' But it was patently clear that he wasn't. He was heavily flushed, his breathing was laboured and he had one hand pressed to the right side of his chest. 'I caught cold is all. Why the fuss?'

Allan laid one palm on Eugene's forehead and with his other hand grasped his thin wrist.

Eugene tried to shake him off, but Allan tightened his hold.

'Come on, fella.' His voice held a compassion that startled Beth who had half expected irritation or impatience. 'You're running a high fever and your pulse would shame a cattle stampede.'

'So, it's a *bad* cold,' Eugene muttered stubbornly, rubbing his wrist as Allan released it.

'I'd call it incipient pneumonia,' Allan replied. 'You need bed rest and antibiotics, Eugene. We cannot provide either. You're on that plane.' He gripped the Texan's shoulder. 'I'm sorry.'

'*You're* sorry,' Eugene rasped, but a spasm of coughing shook him. When it was over, he wiped his mouth with a handkerchief held in a trembling hand, swaying slightly as he looked up at Allan. 'Yeah, well,' he croaked, 'maybe it's a touch of 'flu. *Dammit,*' he exploded. 'Why couldn't it have held off a couple more days? I've waited years for this. To get so close to the glacier and then——' He broke off. A lump came to Beth's throat at his obvious distress.

'Then waiting a little while longer won't kill you,' Allan replied briskly. 'But the pneumonia might, if you don't get it treated. The glacier will still be here when you're fully fit again. You can come back.'

Eugene's head jerked up. 'You mean that?'

Allan nodded. 'It might not be this year, it depends how soon the snows begin. It might not be this route. But if I can't bring you myself, I'll arrange for you to come with one of my colleagues.'

Eugene seized Allan's hand in both of his and was pumping it up and down, his eyes moist. 'I'm much obliged, much obliged,' he mumbled.

Lucille came bustling over. 'Allan, can you talk some sense into his wilful old man? He——'

'Hush your mouth, woman, and git one o' them youngsters to unload our cases. We're catching the plane back to—whatever the dang place is called.'

Lucille gaped at him, then at Allan.

'Well, git along,' her husband said testily. 'It's what you wanted, ain't it?'

'Sure,' Lucille nodded quickly. 'But you said wild horses——'

'Changed my mind,' Eugene snapped. 'No law says a man can't change his mind, is there?'

'No,' Lucille began, 'but——'

'The cases, woman,' Eugene thundered. But the effect was spoiled as he began to cough and, clearly in pain, clutched at his wife for support.

'Come on, old man.' She put her arm around his waist. 'Take it easy. I'll fix you a hot drink.' As they shuffled away he muttered something. 'OK,' Beth heard Lucille placate him. 'So I'll get Hofi to make the drink. I'll stay with you.'

Allan swung round, making Beth jump. He seemed momentarily startled to see her there. For an instant his expression was unguarded and registered longing, pain and confusion. Then the shutters slammed down. 'Get your things together,' he ordered harshly. 'You are going too.'

CHAPTER TEN

SHE flinched as though he had struck her. Her chin came up. 'No.'

His face darkened and his eyes held a menace that sent shivers down her spine. '*What* did you say?' he demanded softly.

Beth swallowed. 'I'm not leaving. There's no reason for me to go.'

'You're wrong,' he contradicted flatly. 'I don't want you here.' His hooded eyes glittered with an emotion Beth could not identify.

Her tongue stuck to the roof of her mouth and her heart thumped uncomfortably against her ribs.

She prayed for strength, and courage. She had known it wouldn't be easy, but *this* . . .

'You didn't want me here from the beginning, so what difference can a day or two longer make?' She listened with amazement to the calm voice issuing from her own lips. 'As Eugene can't go on himself, my pictures will be doubly important to him. I have a job to do. Besides, I gave my word.' The instant she said it she wished she hadn't. But it was too late.

Allan's expression grew bleaker and his mouth curled in biting contempt. '*Your word?*' he mocked. 'Since when have your promises meant anything?'

Beth sank her teeth into the inside of her lower lip to stop it trembling and blinked rapidly to dispel scalding tears. He was hurt and angry, she reminded herself.

At the sound of raised voices they both looked round.

'No, Momma,' Gaynor protested. 'You're just trying to

spoil it for Rob and me.'

'Gaynor, honey, your Poppa is sick. I need you. There's so much to do. You can't expect me to handle it all by myself.'

Beth discerned a hint of triumph behind Lucille's pleading. Then, to her surprise, Rob broke in. 'Gaynor, I think it's best if you go back with your parents.'

'*Rob*,' Gaynor's eyes widened in hurt and disbelief. 'You can't—you don't mean that.'

'Listen, love,' he gripped her shoulders, 'we'll be arriving at the glacier tomorrow or the day after and you'd be on your way back then in any case. There's no way I can take you on to the ice with me. Besides, your mother and father need you.'

The light went out of Gaynor's face and she looked suddenly much older.

'So, that's it then?' Her voice was strained. 'It was fun, see you around sometime?'

'Oh, you *idiot*.' Rob shook her and her head wobbled. 'No, that is not *it*. I shall be stuck on that glacier for three months, thinking about you every minute, well,' he shot a guilty glance at Allan who shrugged and turned away, 'almost every minute, and missing you like hell. The minute I finish here I'll be on the first plane to Texas and I shall expect you to be waiting at the airport, having missed me just as much.'

'Oh, *Rob*.' Gaynor squealed happily, and flung herself into his arms.

Pressing kisses on to whatever bits of her he could reach, he hugged her close. After a few moments he raised his head. 'I hope when we next meet,' he said to Lucille over Gaynor's shoulder, 'it will be in happier circumstances.'

Lucille drew herself up and Beth tensed. 'Young man, looks like I misjudged you. You just won't take no for an answer, will you? Now there's some mighty fine hotels in our town——' Rob's face stiffened and Beth's heart sank, but Lucille had not finished. There wasn't even the hint of a smile on her plump face. 'But there ain't nothing to beat good home cooking. Now if you got a mind to sample some Texas hospitality, we'd be happy to have you stay as our guest.'

Keeping one arm firmly around Gaynor, Rob extended his other hand to Lucille. 'Ma'am,' he grinned broadly as she grasped it, 'I'd be delighted.' Gaynor threw her arms around her mother.

'Listen.' Hofi hurried towards them. She stopped, tilting her head to one side. 'The plane is coming.'

The next few minutes were all rush and bustle as Gaynor's and Hofi's luggage was unloaded, other bits and pieces fetched from the Land Rovers and goodbyes said.

Rob and Gaynor stood with their arms around one another, talking softly. Lucille fussed over Eugene who grumbled as she fastened his coat and turned up the collar.

'Get Beth's case down too,' Allan directed as Gunnar fastened the ropes.

Beth froze. *He couldn't.*

Gunnar stared at him in surprise. 'Why?'

'All the other women are leaving,' Allan pointed out with cool logic, 'and as expedition leader, I think it would be better if she went back with them.'

'But—my pictures,' Eugene wheezed painfully. 'She ain't finished the job yet.'

Furious, desperate, Beth planted herself in front of Allan. 'Please, you can't do this——' she began, but the roar of the twin engines drowned the rest of her words as the plane circled low overhead and came in to land.

Ignoring her, Allan turned to Gunnar. 'Hofi should have someone with her until you get back.'

Beth's shoulders slumped. With unerring accuracy, he had hit the bullseye. Gunnar's greatest vulnerability was his concern for his wife. Already doubt was clouding the Icelander's bearded face.

To everyone's shocked amazement, Hofi suddenly burst into tears. 'I do not want her with me,' she sobbed, pointing at Beth. She clutched her husband's arm and gazed, wet-eyed and pleading, up at him. 'Last night I had a terrible dream. Maybe it was an omen, Gunnar. Please, don't let her come on the plane. There is Vigdis next door. She will come if I need anyone. Please, Gunnar.'

Openly bewildered by his wife's totally uncharacteristic behaviour, Gunnar stroked her golden head and murmured soothingly in their own language. The glance he darted at Beth was uneasy and apologetic, and she recalled how deeply superstitious Icelanders were. They attached great significance to dreams and believed implicitly in the *hidden folk*, invisible spirits who inhabited enchanted spots which humans had to leave alone.

Beth was as bemused as Gunnar. She had always considered Hofi the most level-headed person she knew. There had been mention of nightmares when they talked together earlier. It had to be her pregnancy. The hormone changes affected some women more than others. Beth felt hurt, just the same.

Comforting his wife, Gunnar looked at Allan. 'You are leader, and my friend. I am respecting that. But I am thinking is better for Beth to stay. She must take photographs for Eugene, and we are still needing a cook. After plane leave, we move fast. Maybe reach glacier tonight. Then she come back with me. But now is better she stay.'

The two men eyed one another, neither giving an inch.

A spasm crossed Allan's features, revealing an inner torment that sent shock tingling through Beth. He recovered instantly, suddenly brisk and businesslike. 'Perhaps you're right. We'd better not keep the pilot waiting.'

But watching him help load the cases as Rob assisted Eugene up the steps, Beth saw the grim set of his jaw, and her stomach knotted.

Thanks to Hofi's odd behaviour she was to stay. But the likelihood of convincing Allan they could build a future together seemed as remote as ever.

As final goodbyes were shouted, Beth hung back, suddenly afraid, but knowing she must go on. While there was still a shred of hope, until Allan told her to her face that he no longer loved her, that there was no chance of a reconciliation, she had to stay.

He had already turned to check the ropes securing the remaining luggage.

Hofi followed a reluctant Gaynor up the steps. As she reached the door and bent her head to duck inside, Hofi half-turned, caught Beth's eye, and gave a huge wink. Keeping her right hand close to her body to screen the gesture, she made a thumbs-up sign, then disappeared inside.

Beth stared at the door as it closed. Had she imagined it? Then Hofi appeared at one of the windows, behind Gaynor and Lucille. There was no trace now of her tears and distress, just a beaming smile as she waved.

Beth's eyes widened. Realising what Hofi had done, she glanced towards Allan. He was watching her. One dark brow lifted and his mouth twisted cynically.

She flushed hotly. 'I didn't know——' she began. He turned away.

Drawing in a deep breath, Beth looked once more at the plane, waving both arms, silently thanking Hofi. The engines roared to full power, the brakes were released and the aircraft gathered speed and rose smoothly into the cloudless sky.

Shielding her eyes with both hands, Beth watched it climb higher and higher. A hand on her shoulder made her jump. It was Gunnar.

'My Hofi—what she is saying—is not like her.' He shook his head, still baffled. 'You are angry?'

Beth felt a rush of affection for the huge, gentle man. 'Of course I'm not angry,' she reassured him. There wasn't time now to explain Hofi's motive for acting as she had. Hofi could tell him herself when he got home. 'I expect it's the effect of her pregnancy. It's a very emotional time for her.'

'Beth,' Gunnar clapped her shoulder with an enormous hand, 'you are nice lady and good friend. I wish for you happiness. Allan is big fool. He no seeing how lucky he is. Is no need you staying with him while he angry. You come in my Land Rover. I am friend. I say nice things, make you smile again.'

'She'll be riding with me,' Allan spoke from behind her. How long had he been there? How much had he heard? There was something in the deep, quiet voice that made the hair on the back of her neck stand up. Gunnar must have sensed something, too, for, after an instant's hesitation, he nodded and started towards his vehicle. Allan called after him in perfectly normal tones, 'Did you pick up a weather report?'

'*Já,*' Gunnar nodded. 'Depression is coming, maybe tonight, maybe tomorrow.'

You can say that again, Beth thought wildly, then pulled herself together. There was no turning back, no room for doubt. *Go beyond reason to love. It is safe. It is the only safety.* The lines, calming, strengthening, floated to the surface of her mind. She could not remember when or where she had read them, but that was not important. They had come when she most needed comfort, and inspiration. She had her armour.

'That settles it,' Allan said flatly. 'We must reach the glacier by tonight.'

A slow grin crinkled Gunnar's eyes. 'Foot down?'

The harsh planes of Allan's face relaxed a little as he grinned back. 'All the way.' He turned to Beth, his smile fading.

'You'd better make some sandwiches and coffee while we check the vehicle over. It's going to be a long, hard drive.'

From the grim warning in his tone, Beth realised he would be making no allowances, and prepared herself for the worst.

Within an hour they were once more under way. The track continued across petrified rivers of lava, but this time there was no slackening of speed. It was only by fastening her seat-belt so tight she could hardly breathe that Beth avoided

being hurled against the unpadded metal door, or hitting her head on the roof. As it was, before very long her insides felt like jelly. She wasn't at all sure that eating had been such a good idea, yet without something in her stomach she would have been even less able to survive the strain. The constant cut and rub of the wide strap soon made her shoulder, collarbone and ribs horribly sore.

Beth gritted her teeth and said nothing, knowing exactly what sort of reception her smallest complaint, no matter how justified, would receive. Clutching her camera tightly, she tried to brace herself against the worst of the bumps.

The tension mounted and Beth waited, helpless. She could feel naked antagonism emanating from the tall man beside her.

Allan suddenly turned his head, his expression stony, his eyes tormented and furious. 'Why the hell didn't you go back with the others?'

This was it. In a way Beth was glad. The waiting had been unbearable. 'I couldn't go with things the way they are between us,' she shouted above the creaks and rattles and roar of the engine.

'Why not?' he demanded brutally. 'Things are pretty much the same as they have been for the past two years.' His mouth was a thin, bitter line.

'No, they're not,' Beth argued. 'I didn't know the full story then.' She felt almost sick with nervousness. This was her one and only chance. She had to get it right. Everything depended on it. 'Besides, no matter what happened then, it's *now* that's important.'

He was silent and appeared to be concentrating on the driving, but she sensed a battle raging within him.

They passed an extinct volcano whose steep, conical sides looked unscalable, then skirted a river which had formed a canyon with a waterfall at one end. The rock along the canyon edges was deeply cracked. The river was slowly, inexorably cutting a wider, deeper course.

Automatically, Beth took pictures. She had not forgotten her promise to Eugene. But for the first time in two years her work was not uppermost in her mind.

Then they hit the sand. A tricky, treacherous surface on which to drive, in some places it formed a thin layer over hard rock, in others, pools of quicksand to trap the unwary.

It was as fine as dust and rose in a thick, choking cloud behind the vehicles. Allan had to drop further and further back to be able to see anything at all.

It was stifling inside the Land Rover as the sun beat down from a cloudless sapphire sky, and dust filled the air despite all the windows and ventilators being closed.

They had both taken off their jackets and Allan had the sleeves of his sweater pushed up his forearms.

Rob was relaying information and directions through the two-way radio at Gunnar's dictation.

For a while, Allan attempted to drive single-handed, holding the microphone in his other hand. But after one narrow escape, almost getting bogged down in the loose, watery sand, he thrust the handpiece at Beth. 'Make yourself useful. Find out why we've just gone past the signposted track.'

Biting back the quick retort that rose to her lips at his peremptory tone, Beth did as he asked. She had to concentrate hard to hear Rob's reply above the interference and engine noise. Suddenly she was aware of the tremendous physical strain this drive was placing on Allan.

'Apparently the old route is impassable because of drifting sand,' she said evenly. 'It's a recent change and there hasn't been time to erect new signposts yet.'

Allan nodded briefly, concentrating on the way ahead. Beth noticed that his hard features were sheened with sweat, and streaked where dust had mingled with the moisture. Strain etched fine lines at the outer corners of his eyes and bracketed his mouth.

Another hour passed and the vehicles ate up the miles.

Conversation was limited to relaying warnings of especially difficult or hazardous stretches which seemed to crop up all too frequently.

Though the antagonism and hint of violence seemed to have ebbed away, the atmosphere was still tense. But it was a different kind of tension.

They had just picked up speed after skirting an area of quicksand. Beth was staring ahead through the windscreen. Just as Allan took one hand from the steering-wheel to wipe the sweat from his eyes, Beth sensed something wrong with the track, and shouted a warning. But it was too late. Even as Allan slammed on the brakes, the Landrover slewed sideways and the back wheels sank up to their axles in the soft sand.

Allan hit the steering-wheel with the flat of his hand, swore briefly and explosively, and got out to inspect the damage, leaving the door open.

Beth jumped out on her side, laid her camera on the seat, and hurried round to join him. 'I'm sorry,' she said, reaching his side, 'I should have yelled sooner.'

Allan rubbed his face, a revealing gesture which told Beth more clearly than any words of the pressures within him. Then, pushing his hands through his hair, he rested them on his hips and glanced at her. 'What made you shout at all? I didn't see anything.'

There was no anger, only curiosity, and Beth battled to control the well-spring of hope. She grinned wryly. 'That was what warned me. No tyre tracks. Gunnar must have turned off sharply to avoid this patch, but before I could get the words out, we were already in it.'

Allan crouched beside the half-buried wheel. Lifting a handful of fine sand he let it trickle through his fingers. Suddenly he looked up. 'No photographs?'

There was an inflection in his voice she couldn't quite grasp. 'I—er——' She shrugged. 'It didn't seem tactful.'

'How are the mighty fallen,' he said quietly.

She held his gaze and allowed herself a self-mocking smile. 'You and me both.'

He looked at her a moment longer and she saw the uncertainty, then he bent his head. 'I guess we'd better start digging.'

'Shall I get Gunnar on the radio and tell him what's happened?'

'Certainly not,' Allan snapped, making her flinch. But when he raised his head she saw the grimace. 'He wouldn't let me forget this.' The grimace became a grin. 'I'd never live it down.'

Beth looked down at him, clasping her hands behind her back, so strong was the urge to reach out and touch.

'You could always blame me,' she offered, her tone light.

Allan dusted off his hands and straightened up. 'No,' he said slowly. 'Not this time.' It took all Beth's willpower to remain where she was. She had laid bare her heart, beseeched him to give their marriage another chance. She could do no more. Now it was up to him. All she could do was wait. He turned away. 'I'll get the shovel. See if you can find something to go under the wheels for traction, will you? Gunnar has all the sacks.'

Slightly light-headed, her emotions tightly reined, Beth looked inside the Land Rover. Seeing nothing remotely useful, she grabbed his parka and her anorak. Thank goodness both sand and tyres were clean and dry.

As soon as Allan had cleared enough sand away, Beth tucked the jackets in under the tyres.

'OK.' She waved him away. 'Shout as soon as you're ready. I'll keep the jackets in front of the wheels.'

Allan shook his head. 'You drive. I'll worry about the traction.'

Beth hesitated. 'But what if I——'

'No buts, just drive. And don't tell me you can't do it,' he added as she was about to argue. 'We both know you can.'

He held her gaze for a long moment.

Beth swallowed. She started to clamber in, then hesitated. 'If it starts to roll backwards——' She stopped, visions of his arms being trapped beneath the wheels drying her mouth and knotting her stomach.

'I've got the shovel, I'll jam that under,' Allan replied with a trace of impatience.

'That won't hold it.' She looked round quickly. There was nothing they could use, except—reaching down she grabbed the metal case containing her spare camera and all the film, and thrust it into his hands. 'Take this, just as a precaution.'

Head bent, Allan stared at the case, then looked up at Beth. 'It's all I have,' her voice was suddenly husky.

His jaw tightened and he turned away.

Beth jumped in, closed the door, wound down the window and started the engine. Her heart hammered fiercely. 'Say when,' she shouted, gripping the steering-wheel and carefully engaging the lowest gear.

She held her breath, then, as Allan's deep voice bellowed, 'When,' with infinite care she depressed the accelerator and eased up the clutch. As soon as she felt the bite she released the handbrake. Clutching the steering-wheel, her knuckles white, she eased the Land Rover forward inch by inch.

It seemed to take hours. By the time they were once more on firm ground, Beth's arms and legs were trembling uncontrollably. Opening the door she jumped out, staggered and almost fell, grabbing the door to save herself.

'I'm all right,' she reassured him quickly as he frowned. He mustn't think she was playing for sympathy.

Allan finished shaking sand from the two jackets and flung them on to the back seat. Bending down, he picked up her case, hefting it in his hands. 'You forgot to empty this.' His voice was rough-edged, shaken.

Swallowing, Beth looked him in the eye. 'I didn't forget,' she answered quietly. 'There just wasn't time.'

Allan passed it to her but didn't relinquish his hold immediately. A smile flickered at the corners of his mouth, but his eyes were uncertain. 'It seems this is getting to be something of a habit.'

'Me bailing you out of difficult situations?' Beth asked innocently.

His eyes narrowed. 'I prefer to call it teamwork,' he retorted.

Beth's throat tightened. 'I'll go along with that.' Somehow she kept her voice light.

Before Allan could reply, the radio crackled and Rob's distorted voice filled the air, asking if everything was all right.

Beth leaned in and grabbed the handset. 'We're fine.' She shot a conspiratorial grin at Allan. 'Had to make a brief stop, that's all.'

'It's all this lurching about,' Rob sympathised. 'You want us to hang about and wait for you?'

With a questioning look, Beth passed the mouthpiece to Allan. She put the case on the back seat, reached across for her camera, and took a quick snap of Allan with his arm resting along the top of the door.

'. . . right behind you,' Allan said and replaced the handset. Beth hurried round to the passenger side and jumped in.

As Allan put the engine in gear, he glanced across at her. He seemed about to say something. Then compressing his lips he turned away and they started forward to pick up Gunnar's trail.

It wasn't that Allan looked at her any more often, nor she at him. He had no choice but to keep his eyes firmly on the faint track left by Gunnar's vehicle, or risk another disaster. Yet, sensing a subtle but definite change in the atmosphere between them, Beth felt a stirring deep within her.

As they neared the slopes of a mountainous ridge, the sand gave way to gravel. Then, huge sharp boulders began to appear on the flat surface.

'Where did they all come from?' she asked in surprise.

'Fallout from the Askja eruption in 1875,' Allan replied. 'Rock and debris landed twenty-five miles away. You want photographs?'

'Oh, yes, please.' She smiled her gratitude. Hope was growing by the minute and in the effort to conceal it, her heartbeat quickened and her palms grew damp.

They pressed on through a layer of fine brown ash and climbed into the highlands. 'The American astronauts trained for their moon-landings up here,' Allan said.

With her own senses so finely tuned and her nerves taut, it wasn't hard for Beth to detect a growing tension in Allan. *Trust me,* she willed with all her strength.

The landscape was wild, rugged and barren, with steep craggy slopes and rushing rivers. While the thought of having to brave the foaming torrents made Beth's blood freeze, it also reminded her of their own hazardous crossing. Twice now Allan had relied on her. She hadn't failed him.

In the event, they did have to cross two rivers. But they were wide, clear and shallow, with beds of firm gravel.

The sun was low on the horizon, a blood-red ball in a flame and gold sky, when they came out of a narrow pass and rounded a promontory. There, straight ahead, stretching as far as the eye could see, lay the immense Vatnajökull ice-cap, glistening pale gold in the evening sunlight.

Beth sucked in a quick breath, dazzled by the awesome beauty and sheer vastness of the glacier. Allan remained silent. Without waiting to be asked he stopped the Land Rover.

Forgetting her stiffness and aching muscles, camera already focused, Beth jumped out.

From the main body of the glacier a massive tongue of ice flowed down a valley of volcanic lava, ending in a towering blue-white cliff. Its base was honeycombed with fissures and caves. They looked to Beth like gaping, toothless mouths. Steam hung in a swirling mist above rivers that flowed out from under the ice across gravel wastes dotted with sulphur-edged cones also emitting clouds of steam and gas. The pools of bubbling mud reminded her of Namaskard.

Absently, Beth rubbed her arm. The grazes had healed and she had removed the bandages. But though the bruises had faded to green and yellow, they still showed clearly on her skin.

Lowering the camera after one final shot, Beth got back into the Land Rover, and realised with a sickening jolt that they had come to the end of their journey.

Reflex made her glance at Allan. Arms outstretched, his hands gripped the top of the steering-wheel. Staring straight ahead, his features were set as if carved from stone.

Beth's heart was in her mouth. He had saved her life at Namaskard. He had bathed her face and brought her water when she was sick. He had placed the expedition in her hands at the river crossing, and together, trusting one another, they had got out of the quicksand.

'No, Allan. Don't shut me out.' Desperation made her voice a ragged whisper. 'Believe in me. *Please.*'

His head jerked round and she recoiled from the ferocity in his gaze. 'I—I *can't*——' Shaking his head, he restarted the engine and drove at breakneck speed across the gravel.

Skidding to a halt alongside Gunnar's vehicle, he cut the engine. In the sudden silence, his voice was harsh, mirroring the strain etched on his face. 'You wanted photographs for Eugene. When you've got them, prepare a meal.'

'*Allan*——'

The door crashed shut and he strode away towards Gunnar who was busy with a spanner.

Carefully, as though her agony were contained in a fragile bubble she dared not break, Beth got out.

The air was sharp and pungent with the smell of sulphur. Shivering, she pulled on her jacket then, opening the metal case, put two spare films and the flash attachment into her pocket.

'Hi!' Rob's cheerful voice made her start, and she glanced round.

'Beth?' A look of concern replaced his grin. 'What is it? What's wrong?'

She scrubbed the back of her hand across her face to hide her tears, only to realise from the smears that she had managed to turn the thin coating of dust to mud. That was about par for the course. She shrugged. 'Wrong? Me. Life. Everything.' Closing the case she left it on the seat and, stepping back, shut the door.

'Is there anything I can do?' Rob offered, his sympathy deep and genuine.

Beth sniffed and looked up at him, drawing in a deep breath. 'As a matter of fact, there is. What are you like as a cook?'

'Funny you should mention that,' he grinned. 'Egon Ronay has been known to tremble at the sound of my name.' His voice softened. 'Would you like me to fix supper?'

'Those are the nicest words I've heard all day,' she tried to smile through fresh tears. 'Sure you don't mind?'

He spread his hands. 'What else would I be doing? Gunnar has been in touch with the crew on the ice and apparently weather conditions are still OK. He's hoping they'll be here within an hour so that he can be on his way back home. The chap I'm relieving will drive the other Land Rover back.'

One hour. Beth nodded, not trusting herself to speak, and Rob looked away, avoiding her stark misery. She blessed his tact.

'Go and take your pictures,' he said gruffly and gave her a gentle push. 'I'll cover for you.'

For the first time in two years Beth could find no escape in her work. She went through the motions, using up a whole film on the outside of the ice-cliff. After reloading the camera, she fitted the flash. Walking on a high ridge of black gravel which had formed at one side of the steaming water, she followed the river into the glacier through a long, slanting fissure that widened at the bottom.

Beams of mellow light from the early evening sun slanted through cracks and fissures high above her head.

Automatically, Beth pressed the button, capturing fluted ice columns and fat pillars, the sky through a crevasse, and the clear blue-white ice that formed the walls of the huge cavern. But there was no joy in it, no excitement.

The bubble burst and despair overwhelmed her. Sinking down on a flat rock that edged the river, she laid her camera beside her and, hugging her knees, rocked back and forward in an agony of grief. Sobs tore at her throat and chest.

After a while they eased. She felt empty and numb. Gulping and sniffing, she lifted her head. Her eyes were so swollen she could barely see. She couldn't face them all looking like that.

Leaning over, Beth dipped her hand in the water. Smelling faintly of sulphur, it was beautifully warm, and made her realise how hot, sticky and dirty she was from the journey. The hot water was irresistible.

She began to undress. Peeling off her sweater, she winced. Her limbs were stiff and she ached all over. The front of her body, where the seat-belt had bitten and rubbed, was exquisitely sore and she was utterly exhausted.

Leaving her clothes in an untidy pile, she slid down into the gently flowing water. It was like silk on her bruised body. The river bed was smooth rock and the water reached almost to her shoulders.

A great sigh shuddered through her. She cupped water over her face to rinse away the dust and tearstains, then lay back, resting her head on a lump of rock that jutted out from the other side of the stream. High above, she could see the sky through another crevasse. The ice sang softly all around her.

Massaged by the gentle current her muscles gradually relaxed and her eyelids drooped and closed. She became one with the river. Tranquillity pervaded her, soothing away all the stresses and pain. This was a magical place. She was floating . . . floating . . .

Suddenly, water rushed up her nose and into her mouth. Coughing and spluttering, Beth felt herself grabbed and shaken. She could hear a man's voice cursing viciously. Then it changed, and she heard fear as, harsh and insistent, her name was repeated over and over again.

Dazed, gasping for breath, tears streaming down her face, she opened her eyes.

'Thank God,' Allan rasped, his face ashen and contorted, 'I thought——'

Beth blinked, hanging helpless in his arms, trying to gather her wits. Her eyes widened. She was still in the river. So was Allan, *fully clothed*, his hands clamped around her upper arm.

'Wh-what happened?' she gasped. 'Why are you——?' The question tailed off and Beth felt the blood drain from her face at the look in his eyes.

'I thought——' he began, but cut himself short. 'Beth, was it——? Did you——?'

'No!' She shook her head quickly. 'It was an accident, Allan, I swear. I must have fallen asleep. I—I was so tired . . .'

His gaze flickered down and she watched his mouth twist in self-loathing as he glimpsed the large raw patch on her collarbone. He swore softly. 'You never said a word.' He sounded almost accusing.

She shrugged helplessly and a strangled sound, half-laugh, half-sob, tore at her throat. 'It didn't seem like a very good idea.'

'Oh, Beth,' he muttered, and her heart bled at the torment in his voice.

'I love you, Allan,' she whispered.

He shook his head and, with a groan, crushed her to him. Her fingers tightened convulsively on his soaked sweater.

The stubble on his jaw grazed her cheek and she welcomed it, but could not stop the hot tears that welled up and spilled over her lashes.

Feeling them, he was suddenly still. Then he drew back,

and in his eyes she could see the battle raging. His throat worked, then his voice emerged, hoarse and cracked. 'I can't fight you. I need you too much.'

Slowly his head came down and, as his lips touched hers, lightly, then with a desperate hunger too long contained, Beth put her arms around his neck, her need matching his own.

Clasping her to him, his hands, strong and knowing yet so subtle, slid down her spine and over her hips. She sighed softly against his mouth and he lowered her gently into the water.

Some time later, Gunnar's voice echoed through the cavern. 'Allan? The snowcat is coming.'

Allan lifted his dripping head and called back, 'I'll be there in a minute.' He looked down at Beth lying in his arms. She felt a sudden wrench at his expression.

'He's anxious to be getting back to Hofi.'

Beth bit her lip. What about *them*? How long would it be before she saw him again? What would happen now? Should she speak, or hold her tongue?

Allan splashed to his feet and helped her out on to the rock.

She began to shiver violently, more from apprehension than cold.

His clothes clinging wetly to his body, hair plastered to his skull, Allan bent and picked up her shirt and began tenderly to dry her with it.

She grabbed it, holding it against her breasts. He didn't let go. Raising her head, she met his gaze. 'Allan,' she swallowed, 'ab—about the divorce——'

He shook his head. 'No divorce, Beth. Not now, not ever. It was a test. If you had agreed——'

She had been right. 'But I did agree,' she pointed out softly, a glow spreading outwards from where his warm hand, still holding the shirt, rested lightly between her breasts, to charge every fibre, every nerve-end, with joy.

'Yes, you agreed,' he nodded, his mouth twisting ironically, 'in such a way as to make me realise a divorce would be meaningless. But I still tried to fight the hold you have on me. It was only when I saw you lying in the water, slipping beneath the surface—your eyes were closed—I—*God*——' The remembered agony was vivid on his face. 'You'll never know what——' he faltered and looked away for a moment, his throat working as he fought for control.

He ran his fingers down the side of her face, her neck and over her shoulder, as though to reassure himself she was real. 'Forgive me, sweetheart. I've made you suffer these past few days. But—you are sure, aren't you?' The words burst from him. 'I couldn't bear it if——'

Swiftly, she covered his mouth with her palm. 'I've never been more certain of anything in my life. You are my first, last and only love.'

'Beth, oh Beth,' he muttered raggedly and, clasping her face between his hands, he rained kisses on to her eyelids, her cheek and finally her mouth, lingering as she reached up for him, the shirt falling forgotten to their feet.

Gunnar shouted again. 'Allan? You are all right? Is Beth——?'

'Everthing is fine,' Allan yelled back, cutting him off. 'In fact, everything is absolutely bloody marvellous! Get my case down, will you? I need some dry clothes. I—er——' He looked down at Beth, catching her eye as she struggled damply into her trousers. She felt herself blush and tried, unsuccessfully to smother a smile. 'I decided to take a bath.'

'In your clothes?' Gunnar's voice rose an octave.

Pulling her sweater down, Beth glanced up at Allan. The love in his eyes warmed her soul, and their stifled laughter brought fresh colour to her cheeks.

'It was rather a sudden decision. And, Gunnar, while you're up there, get Beth's case down as well.' Allan bent and picked up the camera and the damp shirt, placing both in Beth's hands, then cupped her face.

'My wife will be coming with me.'

Harlequin Superromance

Here are the longer, more involving stories you have been waiting for... Superromance.

Modern, believable novels of love, full of the complex joys and heartaches of real people.

Intriguing conflicts based on today's constantly changing life-styles.

Four new titles every month.
Available wherever paperbacks are sold.

SUPER-1

Harlequin Romance®

Coming Next Month

2977 RANSOMED HEART Ann Charlton
Hal Stevens, hired by her wealthy father to protect Stacey, wastes no time in letting her know he considers her a spoiled brat and her life-style useless. But Stacey learns that even heiresses can't have everything they want....

2978 SONG OF LOVE Rachel Elliott
Claire Silver hadn't known Roddy Mackenzie very long—yet staying in his Scottish castle was just long enough to fall in love with him. Then suddenly Roddy is treating her as if he thinks she's using him. Has he had a change of heart?

2979 THE WILD SIDE Diana Hamilton
Hannah should have been on holiday in Morocco. Instead, she finds herself kidnapped to a snowbound cottage in Norfolk by a total stranger. And yet Waldo Ross seems to know all about Hannah.

2980 WITHOUT RAINBOWS Virginia Hart
Penny intends to persuade her father, Lon, to give up his dangerous obsession with treasure hunting. She *doesn't* intend to fall in love with Steffan Korda again—especially since he's financing Lon's next expedition in the Greek islands.

2981 ALIEN MOONLIGHT Kate Kingston
Petra welcomes the temporary job as nanny to three children in France as an escape from her ex-fiancé's attentions. She hasn't counted on Adam Herrald, the children's uncle. Sparks fly whenever they meet. But why does he dislike her?

2982 WHEN THE LOVING STOPPED Jessica Steele
It is entirely Whitney's fault that businessman Sloan Illingworth's engagement has ended disastrously. It seems only fair that she should make amends. Expecting her to take his fiancée's place in his life, however, seems going a bit too far!

Available in May wherever paperback books are sold, or through Harlequin Reader Service:

In the U.S.
901 Fuhrmann Blvd.
P.O. Box 1397
Buffalo, N.Y. 14240-1397

In Canada
P.O. Box 603
Fort Erie, Ontario
L2A 5X3

Keepsake

Harlequin Books

You're never too young to enjoy romance. Harlequin for you . . . and Keepsake, young-adult romances destined to win hearts, for your daughter.

Pick one up today and start your daughter on her journey into the wonderful world of romance.

Two new titles to choose from each month.

You'll flip . . . your pages won't!
Read paperbacks *hands-free* with

Book Mate · I

The perfect "mate" for all your romance paperbacks

Traveling • Vacationing • At Work • In Bed • Studying • Cooking • Eating

Perfect size for all standard paperbacks, this wonderful invention makes reading a pure pleasure! Ingenious design holds paperback books OPEN and FLAT so even wind can't ruffle pages — leaves your hands free to do other things. Reinforced, wipe-clean vinyl-covered holder flexes to let you turn pages without undoing the strap . . . supports paperbacks so well, they have the strength of hardcovers!

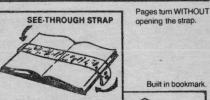

Pages turn WITHOUT opening the strap.

SEE-THROUGH STRAP

Reinforced back stays flat.

Built in bookmark.

BOOK MARK

BACK COVER HOLDING STRIP

10" x 7¼", opened.
Snaps closed for easy carrying, too.